RATNA TRANSLATION SERIES

HAVAN

I0618712

A NOVEL

MALLIKARJUN HIREMATH

TRANSLATED FROM KANNADA BY

S. MOHANRAJ

RATNA BOOKS

Original Kannada copyright © Mallikarjun Hiremath 2001, 2013

First published in English translation 2019
English translation copyright © S. Mohanraj 2019

Illustrations copyright © Basavaraj Gavimath 2001, 2013

ISBN   978-93-5290-751-9 (POD)

Published by RATNA BOOKS
An imprint of Ratna Sagar P. Ltd.
Virat Bhavan, Mukherjee Nagar Commercial Complex
Delhi 110009, India
www.ratnabooks.in

MALLIKARJUN HIREMATH (b. 1946) retired as principal from First Grade College, Hungund. Sri Hiremath lives in Dharwad and has published a collection of poetry, collections of stories, a novel, a travelogue, a collection of personal essays and three collections of criticism. He is a recipient of the Karnataka Sahitya Akademi Honorary Award (2008) among other literary awards. Professor Hiremath is at present the co-editor of *Samahita* – a Kannada literary journal. He has been appointed the president of Basavaraj Kattimani Trust by the Government of Karnataka and has also been working as an Advisor to the Dharwar Sahitya Sambhrama.

S. MOHANRAJ is a teacher of English with more than forty years of teaching experience. He started his career in Mysore and then moved on to Hyderabad for his research in language teaching and teacher education. After obtaining his research degree he has worked in different regions of the country as a teacher educator, materials developer and an education consultant. Professor Mohanraj has been to several countries to deliver talks, teach on their academic programmes, guide research and for keynote addresses at international conferences. He has published books and research articles in a large number of national and international journals.

'*Havan* is about the Lambada people who have been a wandering tribe since ages and who, perhaps, originally belonged to Rajasthan. Literally, *Havan* is the name of a settlement of Lambadas near Kalluru. The novel describes the lives of a few people of this settlement and faithfully recreates the history of the tribe, its characteristic social events and celebrations, songs and dances, beliefs and customs; and their exploitation by landlords and the police. The first part of the novel is narrated by one Basappa who comes to the Thanda (settlement) as a schoolteacher, and the second part is narrated by Loku, Zimri, Hari and Kasanu – members of the tribe.

. . .

'Two streams of thoughts are prevalent in India about the concept of progress among the hundreds of tribes in the country who are culturally rich but suffer from poverty and lack of education. One thought persuades all the communities to join the mainstream by changing their lifestyle, food, clothing, etc., and getting access to modern education and jobs. The other stream argues that the government should provide these people with adequate facilities whereby they can retain their traditional lifestyle as well as food habits and other cultural practices. The first stream is "interventionist" and the second "non-interventionist". Neither the social scientists nor the politicians have been able to decide which of the two is "correct". Both the approaches are not without limitations. *Havan* is emphatic in convincing us that there are no easy solutions to such dilemmas.'

Dr C.N. RAMACHANDRAN
(Excerpt from 'Havana: An Analysis')

To

Jayashree, my wife,
who has inspired me in
many more ways than one

Contents

Part I

One

The Havan Thanda settlement is three-four kilometres away from the village Havan proper. Many years ago, the village chief, Desai, gathered all the people and performed a havan, a fire ritual to propitiate the gods. He assigned the villagers to construct a lake and as a result of that Havan, the lake filled with water to the brim and since then the lake has never dried up. For this reason, the settlement came to be known as the Havan Thanda.

As there is a temple built for Lord Kalleshwara in the village Havan, some of the residents in neighbouring villages call it Kalluru as well. In turn, the settlement next to it is known as Havan Thanda as well as Kalluru Thanda. Somalya is the head of this settlement, so some people call it Somalya Thanda as well.

At one end of the village is a hill, and the settlement is at the other end. If one goes up the hill and looks around, the settlement surrounded by small mounds and hills looks like a small canoe floating on a river.

I have always been interested in the people of the Thanda. When I was a child, I used to look curiously at the Lambada women who often came to our village either to sell fruit or lend a helping hand in harvesting jowar (pearl millet). Looking at them, I would sing the following lines:

Lambani gil gil, wait there wait
Let me join you stop stop.

Occasionally, they would turn back and stare at me. Getting scared, I would clear the place and run away with my friends in tow. Several years later, I got the job of a teacher and was very happy. When people learnt that I was posted to Havan Thanda, they made all sorts of remarks. 'Why do you want to go to that Thanda? You should try elsewhere,' was the advice of a friend of mine. But I could not take that risk. I had no means of trying for other posts. It was impossible for me to let go of this opportunity which had come my way as though accidentally and giving up the hard earned job of a teacher was beyond me.

After having cleared the second year pre-university examination, I had completed my internship while preparing for my BA degree, and thus was eligible for the post of a teacher. But some untoward incidents that took place during my college days resulted in my not clearing the BA examination. I had to stay home. People in the village started looking at me as someone useless. I used to while away my time gossiping or playing cards in the temple porch. I was disgusted with myself. Some of my friends had already got jobs. I often thought, 'If I also get a job, my life will be different.' Though late, I got the job I was looking for. Soon, the attitude of my friends, relatives and the other residents in the village changed. They began treating me with respect. Under peer pressure, I was forced to host a get-together. Sipping his tea, Patil said, 'It is good you got a job, but you should not have been posted to the Thanda.'

'I can do well, no matter what the place is like,' I challenged my friends.

Plenty of thoughts crossed my mind at that moment. 'This is indeed a challenge to me. I'll stay in the Thanda, win the hearts of the people by working sincerely. I'll set goals in my life. I've been given an opportunity to turn over a new leaf.'

One of the senior teachers in my village said, 'Brother, there is one by the name of Somalya Nayak, who is the head of the Thanda. He knows me quite well. Go and meet him and tell

him I've sent you.' These words boosted my spirits. I took some money and the food my mother had packed for me and left for the Thanda.

I got into the bus at Nagarkote, got off at Kalluru, and reached the Thanda on foot. Several thoughts crossed my mind as I walked to the Thanda. How will I spend my days in the Thanda? What will be the type of life there? What kind of people will I meet there? How to motivate the children to come to school?

How do I make myself indispensible to the Thanda?

I was going to a place where I knew no one. This was good in a way as no one would be biased against me. Indeed, this will be an opportunity to start a new life in a new setting.

There were small hillocks on all the sides of the Thanda. The Thanda was nestled on the slopes of these hillocks. The sun had already hid himself behind the hillocks. The sky was crimson, the sheep and the homebound cows raised golden dust.

There were around sixty huts and a few mud-houses in the Thanda. Sevabhai's temple was at the entrance of the Thanda. A few steps away was another temple built for Mariyamma. There was a huge round boulder, perched on it was one more boulder; it appeared as if somebody had carefully placed the huge stones there. The Sevabhai temple encompassed these stones. There seemed to be plans afoot to extend the temple building, as indicated by a heap of stones stacked next to the temple. A white flag fluttered on the Sevabhai temple while a red flag was hoisted in front of the Mariyamma temple. At a little distance from the two temples was a huge neem tree. A circular platform had been built under the tree, beneath its spreading branches. It was here that I sat upon reaching the Thanda on the first day.

I spoke to an old man who sat on the platform making a rope. He was probably hard of hearing. When I enquired about Somalya Nayak, he mentioned some other name and said, 'He will come presently. Everyone will come to the Thanda.' Children who were playing nearby started staring at me with curiosity filled in their eyes. I understood it was time for the people to return home after work and continued to wait on the platform.

Birds flew in from different directions and perched on the tree. The whole tree was soon filled with birds chirping melodiously. I sat listening to the myriad sounds that the birds made. I wondered about the twigs and the branches of the neem tree, spread so wide and strong above the earth and how deep and wide the roots must have sprawled beneath the earth. I watched

the women carrying faggots of firewood, men carrying pickaxes, baskets and other implements and walking home alongside their sheep and other heads of cattle. Within no time, the silent Thanda was abuzz with noise.

A lean old man wearing a short shirt and dhoti came to the platform, sat there dangling his bone-thin legs, turned to me, and asked, 'Who are you, young man?'

'I'm Basappa. I've been appointed a teacher in the Thanda school...Where is the school here? Where is Nayak?' I asked.

'Nayak has lost his senses. He wants the children in the Thanda to go to school because the children in towns go to school. Is it possible for us to learn the way the town children learn? Is it possible for us to dance to the same tunes as they do? We live by hard work. If we send our children to school, we will be left with nothing but mud to eat,' he retorted rather angrily and got up and walked away, muttering to himself.

My very first encounter at the Thanda seemed like a difficult morsel to swallow. 'How rude he is!' I thought. I resolved not to be disappointed with the negative attitude of this man.

As night was settling in, lamps began to flicker in the huts. In my town, electric lights would drive the darkness away. It was not so here. But the stars and the moon that were always hidden there, shone brightly here. The moon appeared like the large kumkum (a red dot placed on the forehead of a woman) on my mother's forehead, while the stars shone like the jasmine flowers she wore in her hair occasionally. They spread cool light all around.

In the meantime, people had started coming towards the platform, the Sevabhai temple, and the Mariyamma temple. A well-built handsome man of about fifty or fifty-five years with a twirled moustache and wearing a yellow turban and knee-length dhoti came up to me and asked, 'Are you the teacher?'

'Yes, and may I know who you are?'

He told me he was Somalya Nayak. I referred to the senior teacher in my town. He said, 'We've built a small room to function as a school not far from here. We'll see to it that you are comfortable. By the way, what do you plan to do for your food? Can I get some rotis for you from my house?'

'No, thanks. I have packed some food from home. It will be enough if you get me some water,' I said. He called the boys playing near the temple and said, 'Go home, get a pot of water and bring it to the school. Bring a lamp and a box of matches as well.' Once the boys returned, we started walking towards the school. A stout man was snoring, leaning against a wall in the veranda of the school. A stench hit my nostrils as the door was unlocked and pushed open. Nayak struck a match and I held up the lamp. A tiny, ant-sized flame swallowed the elephantine darkness!

The boys swept the room and rolled out the mat that was lying in a corner. We sat on the mat. 'It is not necessary to start school tomorrow itself. To begin with, we need to generate interest in the people and the children about the need for education. So don't be worried if things get delayed a bit. If people make negative comments out of their ignorance, don't take it to heart. If you have any problems, do let me know. You should earn the blessings of god by making the children here literate and educating the people,' Nayak said.

'This is my first job. I don't have any experience. But I've come here to work with love and devotion. Please see to it that the children come to school,' I requested. 'Have your food and come to the platform,' said Nayak, and left the place.

I ate the rotis mother had packed with brinjal curry, peanut chutney and onions, drank some water and walked out, belching, on a full stomach. A pi-dog that had smelt the food was lingering around, wagging its tail. I offered it a piece of leftover roti. The man who was fast asleep outside showed no signs of waking up. I started walking towards the platform with the thought of spending a little time there.

Meanwhile, a lot of people had begun to gather at the platform. I reached there at the same time as Somalya Nayak, who came there after his prayers at the Sevabhai temple. A few people sitting on the platform made place for me and said, 'The teacher has arrived.' As soon as Nayak and his friends arrived after offering prayers, women and girls who had gathered there arranged themselves in a circle in the open yard in front of the platform. Nayak came and sat on the platform and introduced me to the people sitting on it. 'Teej (a tribal festival) is close at hand. Girls will be taught to sing and dance as a preparation for the festival,' he said, pointing towards the women. He introduced most of the girls – Gowri, daughter of Kasanu; Zimri, his own daughter; Chandri, daughter of Khemli; Lacchi, daughter of Dhulya; Rukki, daughter of Duglibai; and Gomli, daughter of Khubya. Ruplibai, Somalya's wife, sang and demonstrated the steps of the dance to the girls. Lalibai, wife of Kasanu, was keeping rhythm by clapping her hands and encouraging the girls.

tijeri ouldi kamrayija
kamrayija saari raath keelo dhalkoja
maari saathnooro moondoo kamrayija
kamrayija saari raath keelo dhalkoja

'What does this mean?' I asked Kasanu, who was sitting by me. He explained, 'Uprooting a sapling grown in pots is as painful as

plucking flowers from the creepers. The girls are singing that it makes them miserable. At the beginning of Teej, girls sow wheat and take care to see them sprout. On the final day of the festival, they pull out the saplings and sing this song.' Somalya added, a little meditatively, 'These little girls, who are like the saplings and flowers, have to get married and go to their husbands' houses and live with the mother-in-law, accepting the whole family as their own, isn't it, master (teacher)? The seeds that have been sown here need to be uprooted by the parents and replanted in that place; this is how life is, master.' Having said this, he went into a pensive mood.

The women sang the song and the girls repeated the same, dancing in a circle. As I sat in the moonlight witnessing the dazzle of the tiny mirrors on their skirts amidst the sound of giggling and the jingles tied to their ankles, I was transported into a different, magical world. The moon was delighted to see the girls dance with grace and elegance. The combination of their rhythmic song and dance and the bright moonlight enchanted me. But the chit-chat on the platform was a constant distraction.

Kasanu and Somalya began to talk. 'Your daughter Gowri is still young. My daughter Zimri has come of age two years ago. My wife has been after me to look for a groom. I want to look for a good match from a good thanda, but she insists on marrying the girl to a boy who is related to her. Of course, her brother is handsome and good to look at, but he has to live a life by hard work. If I can give her in marriage to a wealthy family, there will be much less to worry about.'

'Let's ask Dhadi when he comes to the Thanda this time. He keeps visiting all the thandas, he would be aware of good grooms,' said Kasanu.

There was another bit of conversation in progress elsewhere. 'There cannot be another thanda as poor as ours. Other than Somalya and Kasanu who have a couple of acres of dry lands, nobody else possesses anything. We put in a lot of labour every day. We are not left with even a few coins at the end of the day. How can any money be saved after we spend it on festivals, marriages, clothes and sundry items?' Hearing Dhulya's words, Somalya's attention turned from his personal problems to those of the Thanda. 'We will consider cultivating the grazing grounds that have been lying idle here,' he said. In response, Khubya said, 'How can we cultivate the grazing grounds? Will people from Kalluru keep quiet?' Kasanu retorted, 'How is it useful to them? What is wrong in making use of the land that is lying waste?' An old man who was puffing on a choota (pipe) and coughing said, 'Let's not desire things that don't belong to us. We work as labourers on road construction; we work on farms and also build houses. Let's make ends meet with what Sevalal has bestowed on us.'

'Where are the grazing grounds?' I asked.

'A small stream flows down the last hillock. It flows down and collects in the form of a lake. It is not really a big lake, but Desai, when he was building a lake for the village also built a bund for this with a few stones such that some water is stored. Next to it is a piece of land of about two to three hundred acres which is used as grazing grounds. But no cattle go there to graze. The lake in Kalluru is huge. One of its canals reaches the edge of these grazing grounds,' Somalya explained.

'In that case you can cultivate it,' I said.

'I am of the same opinion. But several people advise me not to take on additional burden. I believe Kalluru people have never ever given a thought to this,' said Somalya.

Much discussion on various topics was in progress on the platform. Because I had walked all the way from Kalluru to the Thanda, I was tired and nearly dozing off. Somalya noticed this and bade me goodbye saying, 'Master, you go and sleep. There will be a man sleeping in the school veranda. Bolt the door from inside and sleep.' I went back to my house and in the dim light of the lamp spread my carpet on the floor and lay down after locking the door from inside as he had instructed. It was a new world. I wondered if I could serve the people of the Thanda to the best of my abilities.

Two

The chirping of sparrows that had entered the room through the open window woke me up. I opened the door and found the man who was sleeping outside had already woken up and left. I completed my ablutions and had some rice flakes which mother had thoughtfully packed for me. I lit the stove and made some tea. By the time I stepped out, it was already nine in the morning. I sat on the veranda of the school expecting some people to come there. Not a single soul passed by. I thought of taking a stroll in the Thanda to look for some children and fetch them to the school. The Thanda was more or less deserted. Everyone had gone out to work. Only the very old, some lazy louts, and a few children were left behind.

On the way, I peeped into a hut and saw a man. 'Who is there?' he enquired.

'It's me, teacher Basappa,' I said. 'Yesterday people had been talking about a teacher who has come to the Thanda. Is that you? Come in, come in, please, and be seated,' he said. A very old and wrinkled woman who was mending a blouse with great concentration diverted her attention towards me. 'Not a single child came to the school. I thought I would find out why. I couldn't see anyone,' I said.

'What can be done? We need to work. Unless everyone in the household works, we cannot fill our bellies. It will be difficult to make ends meet. Our people are indeed hard working. But how can we help ourselves? We have plenty of children; we have many festivals and celebrations; there are weddings in the Thanda; besides, we have our vows to gods and saints; we need to meet a lot of expenses,' said the old woman, listing out their woes.

'Somalya Nayak had promised to send a few children to the school. But this morning not a single child came to school,' I reported.

'Somalya Nayak is a very strange fellow. Both his children went to school in Kalluru and are now studying in a bigger school in Nagarkote. Can everyone send their children to school like him?' complained the old man. His wrinkled face showed behind his overgrown silver beard and moustache. As he spoke, the deep lines on his forehead became deeper.

The old man, who had a great desire to talk, looked like a saint. I too felt like talking to him. Curious to know the history of the Thanda I asked, 'Ajja, how old is this Thanda?' He appeared to be waiting for a cue. He cleared his throat loudly and began his narration.

'It is said we belong to the Rajput community from Rajasthan. Our people joined the Mughal troops as soldiers and wandered along with them towards the Marathi and Kannada regions. These people were trading lavana. Do you know what lavana is? Salt. Since they sold lavana they came to be known as Lamanyas or Lambanyas. They also supplied gunpowder, ammunition and food grains. You know to who? To the soldiers, soldiers who were engaged in war on the battlefields. This business was put to an end sometime later, and these people became homeless wanderers. My grandfather used to say that one group of people came to Solapur after travelling to different places. We roamed around the place for several years in search of livelihood and grazing lands for our cattle. We reached Gulbarga and from there travelled towards Badarbandi in Koppal. We settled there. When our group left that place and started on their journey towards Nagarkote, the British flags were lowered and the green, white and orange flags were being hoisted over all the monuments. Around that time everyone was raising slogans – "Bharat mata ki jai!" "Vande mataram!" "Jai hind!"

'When we reached Nagarkote and settled here, luck opened its doors for us. We got the news that Desai of Kalluru was on the lookout for workers to work on the farmlands. Hearing this news, Somalya Nayak's father Manya Nayak, his wife Haansibai, myself, and this old woman here met the first Desai. He asked us to get all our people to make our homes near the town. "We have several acres of land," he said, "you can work on those lands." At that time, we were a group of thirty families staying together in one place. We reached this place with our cattle. We liked this place immensely and decided to live here.

'I said we came from Badarbandi in Koppal. Badarbandi was also a nice place to live in. A major incident made us leave Badarbandi. You could even say that luck was not in our favour. Vasappa, a clerk of Desai, coveted Haansibai, wife of Manya Nayak. The clerk would mount a neighing horse and come trotting to our settlement for inspection. During the harvest, we would all be in the fields guarding the crops at night. In the moonlit nights, the women would be busy singing and dancing while binding sheaves. Vasappa, who came for inspection, gazed at the women folk like a hungry dog. But I never thought such an incident would take place. Vasappa asked for fodder for his horse to be delivered at his house located in the farm. Who was asked to do this job? Haansibai. After delivering the fodder, when she was about to return, he grabbed her by the hand. She tried her best to escape, but all her attempts were futile. Vasappa, who was in a drunken state, somehow managed to hold her firmly and close the door. What a strong person she was! She had plenty of courage and strength. She was someone who could not be subdued by four men. "You bastard! Scum of the earth! You want to have me?" So saying, she gave a forceful kick to his thighs. Vasappa fainted and fell down with a thud. Because of the force with which she kicked him, his head hit against a pillar and blood started gushing out of his head. Haansibai was trembling with rage when she came and narrated all this. She thought he was dead and was filled with such fear that she broke into a cold sweat. She pestered Manya Nayak, "Let us vacate this place. What a terrible place! I don't want you people to suffer on account of me. Let us not stay here, let's go!" Before dawn, my wife and I also joined them to leave the place. Back then, Haansibai was like Jaggur Jamani, a born leader among our folk.'

'What does jaggur jamani mean?' I asked, not able to contain my curiosity.

'Jaggur Jamani is not an ordinary woman. Listen, I will tell you. She was a great leader of our community long ago. A very courageous woman. She would visit the ten thandas nearby, in her command and dispense justice. Once, when she was returning to her thanda on horseback after dispensing justice in another settlement, the Badshah sent his men to capture her and bring her to him. She dismounted the horse in the presence of the Badshah and sat in style. As she sat down, her large skirt puffed up with the air trapped inside. Seeing this, the Badshah mockingly said, "Take care, a rabbit may enter." Listen to her bold and courageous repartee – "If you have the attitude of a dog, a rabbit can enter." The cunning Badshah was coveting her. He saw that her horse's organ was erect and remarked, "Your horse seems to want something." To this she replied, "It is asking you, the Badshah, to come and shake it." Jaggur Jamani wasn't an ordinary woman. The Badshah was pleased with her courage and wit. He sent her back after duly felicitating her. She was a brave woman, our Haansibai. She fell ill and died about seven years ago. She doted on her only son, Somalya Nayak. After he got married, there were a few petty quarrels between her and the daughter-in-law. After the death of her husband, she managed the show as a leader till her son grew up. Haansibai was someone who dispensed justice with utter impartiality.

'After about four years of getting settled in the Thanda, Manya Nayak breathed his last. He was a man with a good sense of humour. He was a spendthrift. All the money he had would not be sufficient to meet his needs. He was active, wise, but luck was not on his side. Sometimes, he would be completely drunk and immobile for days. Haansibai would have to take care of everything. Somalya was the only child that survived after three infants died. He grew up taking care of the Brahmins' cattle. He learnt to read and write in a modest way. Likewise, my son Kasanu can also manage to read and write. He can sign his name. Now a few boys have started going to school in the town. Most people here are illiterate.'

Having said all this, the old man turned towards the old woman, 'A new teacher has come to the Thanda. Will you make some tea for him?' The old woman put aside the blouse she was mending and got up slowly, heaving her entire body weight on her knees. 'I have just had my tea. Don't make tea, I have to leave now,' I said.

'In that case let's not have tea. Let's sit quietly for a while,' the old man said.

'I'll tell you about our Lambada tribe. Listen to this story. The Lambada tribe is not an ordinary tribe. Several great people were born in this tribe, but look at our state now, what we have been reduced to. Our progenitor was Mola. He was a bachelor. Though his brothers got married, he was happy tending cows like Lord Krishna. He lived his life devoting it to the service of god. As days passed, he was worried about the continuation of the clan. Radha was pleased with his devotion; she wanted his clan to grow without affecting his celibacy. She summoned the kings and barons in the area and ordered them to send a boy from each of their kingdoms. They all agreed, and the kingdoms of Chougadha, Paagadha and Ramgadha each sent a boy to Radha. Radha gave these three boys to Mola to adopt as his sons. Since then, three clans have emerged among the Lambadas known as

Chavhan, Pawar and Rathod. Mola, who worked as a cowherd, was a noble man. You should also know about another great man called Sevalal. His story is an intricate one. As one narrates, several stories roll out. It is like the long turban worn by the Marwaris. Let's stop here for today.'

'I am also interested in knowing all the details. It was engaging and the time was well spent. I think Nayak will come home only in the evening,' I said. 'Yes. This chief of ours, Somalya Nayak is a great devotee of Sevalal. A very gentle person. He is not like his mother in dispensing harsh justice. He does not get drunk like his father. He always keeps himself busy with work. He respects our culture and customs. He confides in the elders when taking decision in matters of administration. He is keen on the development of the Thanda. If educated people like you join hands with him our troubles are likely to end.' I wanted to take leave, but the old man continued. 'I have lost my strength. Every day, just the two of us – the old woman and I – sit here. The children and grandchildren go out to work. It was good of you to have come here this morning. This woman and I, we have suffered a lot, we have also had our good days – that's a different matter. When the time comes, this body made of flesh and bones will collapse. None of us have come into this world to stay here permanently, but the few days we are here, we should be useful to our fellow beings. Sevalal must have sent you here, it must have been His wish.' The old man revealed his philosophy of life and expressed his confidence in me. 'Ajja, may god bless you with a long life,' I said, and left the place.

Old people like him are the historians of this Thanda. They have been transmitting traditions to the next generation and fortifying it. He not only told me about the nomadic settlers of this Thanda, but also gave me information about Somalya, his mother, father, Jaggur Jamani and Mola, the progenitor. In some ways, he had drawn my attention to the invisible roots of the Thanda. The roots remained invisible, but had the strength to anchor a huge tree.

It was necessary to know about the lives of people, while attempting to unravel the history and traditions of the Thanda. I got curious to know the past, present and future of the people. If I could be of some use to this community as I watched them develop and participate in their progress, my life would have served its purpose.

Three

In the evening, I took a stroll towards the hills. The ember-like sun had already begun to take shelter behind the hills. Jumping over tawny rocks on a hillock of mud and boulders was relaxing and enjoyable. The breeze was cool. I was at peace. A small meandering stream made its way between the boulders, occasionally jumping from small heights and rushing with a gentle murmur towards the slopes to form a lake. Frogs perched around the lake were quacking and drawing the attention of their mates. A snake in between the rocks had partially swallowed a frog. Just the two legs were visible, sticking out of the snake's mouth. On a nearby tree was a small eagle. Small fish were scampering in the water while the larger ones moved about slowly in a dignified manner. They would taunt the small fish once in a while, as they tried to escape deftly. White egrets were flying out of the lake in flocks. On the other side was the sprawling green pasture.

Grass appeared to be making attempt to sprout from between the rocks and mud. One could see plenty of berries of different types growing in shrubs. While some Lambada women had gathered berries in small baskets and were getting ready to go back, others had collected firewood into faggots and carried them on their heads as they were walking down the slopes of the hills. The boys were merrily jumping and driving the cattle back home, joyously shouting, 'haale, haale, haale!' Butterflies and bees were buzzing around a host of nameless flowers. The entire hillock was breathing in their fragrance. As I was taking the next step, a fat snake crept under the rock, hissing. I wandered around and got back to the Thanda as it was beginning to get dark. Lamps lit in the huts of the Thanda looked like a huge swarm of fireflies. One could hear the mooing of the cows and the bleating of the sheep. Petty quarrels and swearing among the folk who had just got back from work were ensuing. I reached the platform and sat on it. The birds were chirping on the tree when a huge eagle-like bird perched there. Other birds got unsettled for a while and flew back again to their nests.

Slowly, the people started coming towards the platform. Some of them sat in front of the Mariyamma temple, a few others sat in front of the Sevalal temple and the rest proceeded towards the platform. As they were sharing their day's events with others while puffing on their choota, three drunken men came swaying into the place. 'They have emerged from Duglibai's hut after a few drinks,' said a man to another. Two of the drunkards took the road to Kalluru, shouting and walking unsteadily. The third came towards the platform. 'This drunkard, Damla, brought two customers from Kalluru, so Duglibai has given him a free drink. This rascal drinks and misbehaves,' said Kasanu. 'Do you know who this Damla is, master? The one who sleeps in the veranda of the school.'

I had never looked at him from close quarters; even now, his face was not clearly visible, but it was the same stout figure. When he advanced towards the girls who were dancing, they moved aside, saying, 'Damla uncle is here, make way for him.' When he playfully went near the girls in spite of that, the others complained, 'Leave them alone, why do you trouble them? There is no limit to your drinking.' When Rukki teased him by addressing him as 'pot-bellied uncle,' he held her by the hand and tried to pull her close to him. She wriggled herself free and ran away. 'Dance, dance merrily. I am here to witness your dancing and singing.' So saying, he also began to sing loudly and dance.

Getting disgusted with him, the girls quietly cleared from the place.

People seated on the platform started making fun of Damla. When one of them said, 'Come here, on this side,' he stumbled towards the platform and tried to flex his muscles in a manly way. 'All you elders of the place, "man dekhan howsocho kaayi." What do you think of me? Do you all know that Jangi and Bhangi, the brave leaders of our clan were the right and left arm of Asaf Khan Wazir? I am an incarnation of that brave leader, Jangi. I will also acquire lands like Jangi and own thousands of heads of cattle. This is my word, keep watching!' So saying, he broke into song –

> *ranjankaa paaniv*
> *chapparakaa phaas*
> *dinme theen khoon maaph*
> *aur jahan asaf khan ke ghode*
> *vahan jangi bhangi bail khade.*

> No barriers for us
> For the waters that belong to Sardar,
> For grass to thatch the roofs;
> The oxen of Jangi and Bhangi stand firm
> Where the horses of Asif Khan are tethered
> Bold and brave not frightened of anything.

He kept shouting, 'I have a right to do whatever I want. I will have a drumful to drink, who are you to question me?' Nobody sitting on the platform took him seriously. Someone taunted him, 'See how the grandchild of Jangi is making a scene!' Someone else dismissed him, 'Though he hardly has a few sheep to tend, he dreams wild dreams and claims to be Jangi's grandson, this scoundrel.' This great descendant of Jangi started walking towards the school unsteadily. Kasanu turned towards me and said, 'You don't need to get frightened of him. Though he shouts and picks quarrels when he is drunk, the rest of the time he is sober and behaves well. Now he will go and sleep, and that's the end of it.'

By the time Somalya finished offering his prayers and came to settle himself on the platform, this incident had come to an end. Once again, the girls and women were gathering to practise their singing and dancing. I wanted to quietly draw his attention to my problem. 'Not even three or four children came to the school. If the education officer comes to inspect, how do I explain the situation?' I said. Somalya responded, 'We've had a discussion. My daughter, Zimri, Kasanu's younger son and daughter, Damla's son...in all, around six to seven children will come to the school from tomorrow. Some of our girls and boys are grown up. But none of them are literate. Treat them as young children and teach them.'

I told him about my wandering around the Thanda and having met an old man and talking to him. 'Yes, after I washed myself and had tea, I met Kasanu's father, Ramji uncle. It seems you spent a lot of time talking to him. I call him uncle. Ramji is an elderly person and we all respect him. He is not educated, but a wise man. When we were young, it was he who told us the stories of the Lambada heroes, saintly men like Mola and Sevalal. He is one who believes in hard work. He says one has to earn food by the strength of his arms. In our view, Ramji uncle is like our progenitor, Mola. He does not like deceit and lies. I used to get engaged in petty thefts with my father. My mother stopped me and sent me to work as a cowherd in a Brahmin's house. It was then that I learnt to read and write in a modest way. My mother never liked my father's way of living – a wasteful life. She desired that her family prosper and the Thanda progress and she dreamt that her son's future be bright. She implanted those dreams in me. She wanted me to work hard and bought a couple of oxen to till the lands. She was very proud of her maiden home; she held her grandfather in high esteem. I recall how she used to praise her grandfather. Her grandfather looked like a Sikh. He wore his turban in the Rajput style. He was tall, sported long hair and wore a shirt tied with strings. Many a time, she spoke about the style with which he smoked the choota and chewed beetle leaves – it was worth watching. When he held the panchayat meeting, he would be strictly objective while dispensing justice and pronounce his judgment in a frank and forthright manner. He wore a hemp string around his waist. He tied a lemon to this string. The house was rich with cattle and silver coins. "I, who belonged to such a prosperous family, have now no one to depend on other than you, my son," she would say. "You are the only one surviving after the small pox that took my other children. You survived because you are strong. You should grow up and save the Thanda." These words of my mother still ring in my ears. My mother is not here today, but her memories and words have taken deep roots in me. I also feel, if by the grace of the lord Sevabhai we manage to get some lands, we can harvest gold. When I see these people singing and dancing in the moonlight, I also feel like dancing. But we cannot fill our stomachs by drinking and dancing. For that we need to strain our bodies and work in the hot sun; earn enough to build a house and buy lands; this has been my dream.' Somalya was lost in thought as he spoke, puffing on his choota. I listened to him without interrupting. Then I bid goodbye and walked towards the school. As usual, Damla aka Jangi aka Kumbhakarna was snoring. His belly heaved up and down like the bellows of a blacksmith.

Damla, who had left the place by the time I got up the previous day, was still around that morning. I was a little frightened by his huge form, well-groomed moustache and tall stature. He sized me up once and asked, 'Are you the teacher here?' I sighed in affirmation. 'Lend me ten rupees. I shall return it in four-five days,' he said, without any hesitation. I knew this was a bad loan that would never be returned. I thought of pouring out my woes and saving myself from the situation. 'I have just joined this job,

I am yet to draw my salary. I have borrowed money from others before coming here to join my duties,' I pleaded. His dark face grew darker. He said in a loud voice, 'Look here, master, if you want to work here in peace, give the money I asked for. I haven't asked you for a fortune.' I gathered some courage and responded, 'I am not rich. Though we have some lands, the yield is very little. We also work hard to earn a living.' He cut me short with, 'Whatever it is, take out ten rupees. I don't need your history.' Playing smart and handing over a note, I said, 'Make do with this fiver.' He pressed it against his eyes and left the place.

Four

A t last, ten children started coming to school, though on the rolls were only six. This is because four of the ten children were too young and would come with their brothers or sisters. As days passed, the number increased from ten to fifteen and sometimes touched a high of twenty-five. I had to teach the letters of the alphabet both to the elders and children at the same time.

It was difficult to work with children who wore dirty, stinking clothes. I wondered if the number would dwindle if I started giving lengthy talks on cleanliness and taking baths regularly. Added to this was the problem of language. While the elders spoke Kannada fluently, they conversed with the children in their mother tongue (Lambada). The children did not know Kannada properly. Since some of the grown-up girls – Zimri, Gowri, Gomli, Rukki – knew Kannada well, I could teach the children some words with their help in translation.

It took some time for me to convince the parents about the need to talk to their children in Kannada once in a while. I also proposed the idea of cleanliness and its importance. I learnt that behind my back some severe comments were passed about me. 'If we set aside heaps of work and start giving bath to our children and wash their clothes, who will take care of these other chores?' Such comments spread across the village by word of mouth. It was a comforting thought for those who considered sending children to school a pain. Somalya, Kasanu and I attempted to change their thinking by visiting each and every hut. The situation seemed to improve a bit. But from time to time, children continued to abstain from the school for various reasons.

One day, Rukki, daughter of Duglibai, did not come to school. When I enquired, the other children said, 'Her mother brews illicit liquor. She has gone to Kalluru market to buy jaggery.'

I went to Duglibai's house in the evening, after school. The people who had gone out to work were yet to return. But I could hear people talking loudly inside Duglibai's hut. A young man was busy brewing liquor outside the hut. Liquor drops were collecting in a pot through a pipe attached to another pot which was brewing the hot liquid. The young man was pouring water over the pot to cool it. As soon as he saw me, he said, 'What brings you here, master?' Seeing me at her door, Duglibai's daughter hurriedly disappeared from there. I thought she was filling glasses with liquor. A few people were eating well-baked crisp millet rotis smeared with oil and chilli powder while sipping liquor. One man held out his glass towards Duglibai and said, 'Fill it up, once again.'

'That's enough, you leave the place now,' she ordered.

'How dare you ask me to leave?' The man took out two fivers and threw them at her. 'Will you or won't you fill the glass now?' Duglibai brought liquor in a mug and poured it into the glass. She saw me standing at the door and came up to me. 'My daughter told me that you had come. She ran away dropping the work on hand after seeing you here.'

'She must have been frightened seeing me here because she did not come to school today. She could also have felt embarrassed about the liquor trade in the presence of her teacher,' I said. The drunkards were quarrelling with each other inside the hut and one fellow was tugging at the other. The other fellow bared and slapped his thigh and challenged his attacker to a fight, 'Come, let me see. You seem to want to fight with me. You are becoming increasingly intolerable. Come out, let me see, I will give you a fitting reply. You bastard, come out.'

'Lachamanna, please pacify those fellows inside. I will come after I finish talking here,' Duglibai said. Lachamya, who was tending the fire under the pot and brewing the liquor, went in, threatened them, cajoled them and tried several tricks to make them keep quiet.

A small child began to cry inside the hut. 'Wait, I will come back in a minute,' she said and went in and came back with the child in her arms. She put the child in her lap and gently dandled it, trying to calm the child in vain. She sat in front of me, bared her generous breast, and started breastfeeding the child. Once the child calmed down, she said, 'Bad boy, my breasts are dry, but he sucks on them as a matter of habit.'

'Is this child yours?' I asked.

'Oh god, no. It has tagged on to me for the last one month. Its mother suffered a heat stroke and died. She had lost her husband earlier. What can be done! As the saying goes, "Children of the dead fall into the lap of the living." I am protecting the child. If a life takes birth on this earth, saving it is the responsibility of the humankind. Isn't that so, master? I am feeding him goat's milk. Let him survive. He will share whatever food we have with us; if we starve, he will also have to starve.'

'I came to ask you not to stop Rukki from attending school.'

'What can I do? I have this business; when it is brisk, I have to ask her to leave school. My family has been in this business for generations; when we have customers from Kalluru, the business is good. I have been in this business since the days of the Manya Nayak.'

A jeep drove up to the hut in full speed and stopped abruptly in front of it. A few khaki-clad men got off the jeep, walked into the hut with heavy treads and broke the pot that was brewing liquor with their batons. They ransacked the entire place, throwing everything out – the bottles, glasses, mugs, and the sal-ammoniac. Duglibai pleaded with them, 'Please leave the poor people alone. Don't snatch away their bread. I will give you something if you want.' The customers dispersed and ran for their lives.

'I am the school teacher here; I am going from house to house requesting the people to send their children to the school,' I told the policemen, when asked. They then hit Lachamya and Duglibai a couple of times with their batons and asked them to get into the jeep. Duglibai got into the jeep crying and pleading. Three or four other Lambada women were also taken inside the jeep. The girl, who was hiding in the house, came out and started crying. I was at a loss for words. The jeep sped away towards the hills.

Later, they made the Lambadas locate the pots of liquor hidden in the forest and destroyed all of them. The excise contractor in Nagarkote had informed the department and sent them to raid the Thanda. The Lambadas who were taken in the jeep were thrashed and made to undertake an oath not to continue brewing the liquor.

That evening, people did not gather near the platform. The Thanda was trembling with fear as if it had been plundered by armed dacoits. I went straight to the school.

Khubhya came to the school later that evening. I was taken aback by the incident and narrated to him the entire episode. 'Duglibai was led astray by her husband. This business appealed to them as there was a daily flow of cash. In his greed for money, he allowed his wife to sleep with customers inside, while he himself slept outside the hut. How do we account for such people's behaviour? This girl who attends the school was born after her husband's death. Members of the panchayat in the Thanda had excommunicated Duglibai. But after her husband died, some of the elders took pity on her and said, "A lone woman, let her come and stay in the Thanda." Besides, if she stayed out, they suspected she may shamelessly continue to solicit men. We therefore admitted her into the Thanda once again. You seem

to be badly affected by this. She is used to all this,' explained Khubhya.

'Damla has not been seen for a few days,' I said.

'His is a long story. You will come to know by and by.'

'He borrowed five rupees from me,' I said.

'Master, do not give him any money in future,' he cautioned me. 'He must have gone on a long journey.' He sat on the school veranda, smoked a choota, and left, saying, 'I'll see you again.'

Five

gangninagowri aayicharloko
hum banjaaraviya jaanako
nali bharaila toplali bharaila
hum pardesi saarudaavo
laalbharvaa ayere

Gowri and Ganga have arrived
To be with us the Banjara folk
Our houses and granaries are full
We aliens are here to help
Come to fill the granaries

The entire Thanda was soaked in the mood of Teej festivities. Friends, relatives, and others had come from various settlements in the surrounding area. A majority of the visitors were youngsters.

During these nine days, the girls wake up before dawn, take a bath in the wellwater, and, wearing wet clothes, carry pots of water to the temple to water the saplings kept there. I witnessed this ritual on all the nine days. During this period, the girls eat bland food and take care of the sapling that belong to them. The girl whose sapling is the brightest green is considered to be the most pious of them.

The saplings in Zimri's pot were green and Ruplibai felt happy for her daughter. Zimri and her friends did not come to school for these nine days. I used to get details of their saplings from other girls. Zimri bore a striking resemblance to her mother. She had a very attractive build with good features. When she stood by me as she wrote the letters of the alphabet on her slate, I used to feel a strange sensation. The school appeared desolate in the absence of these senior girls. I was waiting for the day they would return to the school.

There is a folktale about the origin of Teej. Sri Krishna forgets to tend his cows while playing in the river with Radha and other gopikas. Later, when he remembers them, he goes in search of them. Despite looking for them for eight days, he does not find any trace of them. As he is on his way home, disappointed, he spots cow dung. He discovers small saplings sprouting out of the cow dung. Sri Krishna asks, 'Who are you?'

'I am Bhagirathi,' was the reply he got. Bhagirathi offered to help Sri Krishna look for his cows by acting as his guide, and with her help he located all of them. In honour of Sri Krishna finding his cows, the day is observed as the sapling day or Teej.

On the ninth day of Teej, the Dhamboli pooja was performed with grandeur. Though the girls danced the whole day, carrying pots on their heads, they still appeared fresh. Their bodies were as flexible as the tender saplings. The dance and their bearing was a feast to the onlookers' eyes. Zimri, lean and tall, looked charming. Rukki, though she was not tall, was still attractive, with her lovely, deep eyes and eyebrows that were shaped like sliced mangoes. When she laughed, there were dimples on her chin. The tenderness of the growing saplings was reflected in these girls. They were naturally beautiful, like the flowers that grow in the wilderness. Watching the girls dance, one wondered if the deity of the forest had assumed several forms and was dancing there.

Once, when the girls went to collect mud to make male and female dolls – 'ganaghora' and 'ganaghori' – the boys began to tease them. Zimri was being closely followed by her mother's younger brother. When she called him 'ganaghora' light heartedly, he responded by calling her 'ganaghori'.

Ruplibai had invited her brother home for the festival with a purpose. She strongly desired to maintain the bond with her parental family. But since they were very poor, Somalya was of the opinion that his daughter may not be happy if she was married into that house. Though Somalya looked a little upset that day, the mother and daughter were in high spirits.

Rukki, Duglibai's daughter, was being closely followed by Lachamya of Kalluru. Rukki was attracted to him as he used to fetch odds and bits for Duglibai from Kalluru market. Moreover, he had stood by her during raids by the excise department and saved her with his presence of mind. Lachamya accompanied the girls when they went to the lake bed to fetch mud for making dolls. He hovered around Rukki and the two of them tried to share a private moment behind some bushes. Limbya noticed this and he and his friends surrounded the two of them. The two were caught and produced before the elders of the Thanda. Limbya began shouting loudly, 'It has become easy for outsiders to come to the Thanda. They are encouraged by our girls who are ready to loosen their frills for them.'

Duglibai used to ask Rukki to serve liquor in her hut. It was a common sight to see youth from Kalluru visit Duglibai's hut and return unsteady and swaying, in a drunken state. Rukki enchanted them with her looks. Duglibai was careful with her daughter and kept a close watch over her. She never allowed the drunken noisy men to go near her daughter. However, she kept quiet when she moved about freely in the company of Lachamya. Though in the open she said, 'He is a nice boy and comes to our house,' in her heart of hearts she desired that Rukki would marry Lachamya who owned a piece of land and was also very supportive of her and her trade. 'How can Rukki be happy if she marries a man from our own community who has no means of earning a livelihood?' she thought.

Rukki was influenced by her mother and was aware that Limbya was a well-built, strong man. But Lachamya was given to wearing trousers and shirts like fashionable people. He had promised her many luxuries. He said, 'Let us get married and go away to Nagarkote. We can watch movies every day and you can wear beautiful saris.' Her mind constantly tossed between Limbya and Lachamya and finally she chose Lachamya. Rukki's fair complexion and charm had always mesmerized Lachamya.

When Limbya learnt that Rukki was attracted to a man from a different caste, he felt slighted and jealous. When he caught Lachamya and Rukki together and brought them to the village elders, Somalya released them both with a remark, 'Let us not precipitate the matter now; we will discuss this later in the panchayat.' After this incident, the hopes and aspirations of other girls suddenly began to fade away like the young saplings of Teej plucked from the pots.

Teej was concluded in a hurry. Somalya gifted one rupee to each of the girls who had sown the seeds and cared for the saplings. As he pulled out the saplings, he wished for kaslath (well-being and happiness of newlywed couples).

panch panchat raja bhojera sabha
sagal kacheri raameri
ayi bhagirathi vanspateti
daav saanena haro chunga ghalo
sagan bhayi se kaslath.

In an assembly resembling the court of Raja Bhoj,
In the generous panchayat named after Sri Ram,
Bhagirathi coming from green vegetation, spreads happiness
Let me share these green saplings with the elders
Wishing every living Banjara health and happiness.

'Bhagirathi, who rose from the Vanaspati, has given us all

happiness. I shall pluck the saplings and give them to all the elders assembled here.' So saying, he distributed the rich green saplings. The girls sang the song with a note of sadness as they pulled out the saplings they had tended so lovingly.

teejeri oldi kamraayija
kamraayija saari rath
keelo dhalkhoja

As the flowers separated from the creepers
Fade and wither away
Plucking the saplings tended for nine days
With love and care
The faces of these girls
Fade and wither away.

The girls pulled out the saplings, gave them to each one of the elders assembled, and bowed down to touch their feet in respect.

Six

Somalya invited me to his house during Teej. The preparations for the festivities were happening on a grand scale. I stood on the porch which was washed with cow dung and appreciated the dotted floral patterns drawn on the walls and floors in the form of rangoli. Ruplibai, who came there to give me a small pot of water to wash my feet, said with a smile on her face, 'These rangolis are drawn by the girl who is your student.' The rangoli patterns, the henna patterns on her hand, and the abundance of bangles on her forearm also seemed to laugh with happiness. The whole porch was spirited. I washed my feet and while returning the pot to her I had a look at her from a very close distance. She was a dignified-looking middle-aged woman who was strong and well-built, with fair complexion. The skirt decorated with tiny mirrors, the blouse, the veil, and the nose ring – all seemed to be proud to be part of her person.

The floor of the house was smeared with cow dung. Goats, cows and oxen were tethered outside the house. It was evident that half the wall had been freshly whitewashed. The grain had been stored in different bundles and the sacks had been covered neatly with sheets. The decorations for the festival made the interiors and the outside of the house look grand.

Zimri brought a small carpet and spread it on the floor for me to sit on. Somalya, who sat on one of the bundles, gave instructions to Zimri and Ruplibai. 'Zimri is good at drawing the floral patterns,' I said.

This made Zimri feel shy, which made her look even more charming. 'Master, in our place the boys are better than girls in drawing the floral patterns. Kasanu and Khubya do this job meticulously during the religious ceremonies and festivals,' Somalya said. These people seemed to be culture and tradition conscious despite their poverty and sufferings.

The skirt Zimri wore was a little longer than required. Therefore, as she moved into and outside the house several times to get us water to drink or plates to eat our lunch on, she held her skirt up. Her agility and brisk movements inside and outside the house while doing various chores added life to the house. Clutching her sides, she burst into laughter when her uncle whispered something into her ear. When Somalya looked at the two of them angrily with glaring eyes, they retreated to a different place. It is needless to say her eyes constantly followed her uncle.

As per Somalya's instuctions, Ruplibai served me a generous helping of food, with affection. 'Master, we have made some sweets; no meat has been cooked today, so don't have fears about that, and don't feel shy,' was what she said while serving me food. I was moved by their affection and remembered my parents.

I used to visit their house once in a while. Sending two sons to the school in Kalluru and later to high school in Nagarkote and then to college had become possible because of her earnings. She used to sell a variety of berries in Kalluru and neighbouring villages, and when they were not available, she would sell firewood. I was told that when she was pregnant with Zimri, she had carried a bundle of firewood from the hills and sold them in Kalluru. As she was returning home, she developed labour pains. She delivered the child on the road, managed to severe the umbilical cord, and walked home with the newborn child. And in just about four days, she was back to work. A very strong woman, I thought. She was laughing and seemed to be pleased while narrating all her experiences and this seemed special to me.

Sometimes, the couple would engage in mock fights with each other in my presence. 'He married me without even offering me a new skirt,' she teased her husband. 'My in-laws have never invited me to their house and honoured me even once,' was his taunting response. 'My mother-in-law is not an ordinary woman. She has troubled me a lot. She made me suffer a lot. This man used to beat me a lot as a result of his mother's complaints. It is only now that he has tempered down. My parents are very poor people. What can they give?' Somalya would change the course of their conversation as I used to get frightened at the thought of this mock fight turning serious.

I was overpowered by the affection showered on me by this family and automatically all other troubles in the Thanda seemed like trifles.

Seven

The people of the Thanda were meeting on the platform under the neem tree, as usual. The tree that stood in silent meditation throughout the day would become a social being in the evenings with people gathering around and the birds chirping on its branches as they settled down. Excited about its participation in the happy events, the tree would gently nod its head to issue cool breeze. It would also sigh sad notes on listening to the miseries of the people. Upset with their petty quarrels and squabbles, it would stand still, arresting all breeze. Today, it seemed to be expressing anger.

People began to gather under the tree, but there was no social gossip or the everyday chit-chat. The elders sat on the platform and the rest gathered in the open yard. The atmosphere was tense.

Dhaliya had gone to Duglibai's house to summon her and her daughter Rukki to present themselves before the Ghor Panchayat. He had also instructed them to bring Lachamya along. As they came and sat down, everyone's eyes turned towards them. Limbya and his friends were seething with anger. Limbya had met all the elders before the meet and announced, 'The time has come to guard the prestige of the Lambadas.' He was seething with rage, anger, disgust and jealousy as Rukki was slipping out of his hands and wooing a man from another community. Nayak, Dhavo the secretary and other elders were seated on the platform in a dignified manner. It was a matter of curiosity for the rest of the members of the Thanda. Rukki and Lachamya looked embarrassed. However, Duglibai was chewing on her tobacco and spitting out the spittle in a show of bravado to face the questions about to come. Children sat silently staring at the gathering after they were chastised by Dhaliya for making noise while playing nearby.

The secretary made clear the reasons for the meeting of the Ghor Panchayat and continued, 'It is a delicate matter for discussion today. Firstly, our prestige is being sold rather cheaply because of Duglibai. Police have been visiting the Thanda often because of people like her. Though others sell liquor on the sly, Duglibai sells liquor openly with no qualms. Secondly, we are not assembled here to discuss the issues related to our Thanda; Limbya has brought to the notice of the elders the fact that a youth from Kalluru stays with her and has been in a relationship with Rukki. We have to discuss both the matters today.'

One of the elders asked, 'Is this all true, Duglibai?' She responded, 'The whole world knows that I own a liquor shop. There are at least seven to eight other huts where illicit liquor is made. What other means of survival do we have?' When Somalya suggested, "Find some other profession and stop the liquor business," she questioned him with, 'It is easy to suggest. Do you want us to starve by stopping our trade? How can everyone get a job? Even if one finds a job, will that be sufficient to survive? People in the village have money. They come, drink and give us money. How does this affect you?' Others involved in the liquor business supported Duglibai loudly.

At that point, another elderly person introduced a twist to the talks in progress. He made sure that she did not get the necessary support, and brought in the more serious issue of the prestige of the Thanda. He said, 'Our discussion now focuses on finding the truth about your daughter, Rukki, being in love with a boy from the village. Is this true or not? Is it also true that the two

of them went to Kalluru market together? She went with him to Nagarkote; Limbya has told us about how he was constantly keeping company with her during Teej.'

'These are mere lies. Some people who are jealous and do not like us spread rumours of this sort. He is a good boy. He comes home and helps us. That's all,' she was emphatic.

'If your words are true, take a bunch of neem leaves and swear by them,' suggested an elderly person. When a person offered her a bunch of neem leaves and insisted, 'Take these, take these,' she refused to touch them. She stood there, with her head bent.

'Aren't you ashamed? Do you think this is right? Is there no proper match for Rukki among our youth? Perform her marriage in an appropriate manner with one of our own boys,' counselled another elder. Duglibai recovered and said rather strongly, 'Listen to me, all of you elders seated here. I am a simple woman born in this Thanda. I speak frankly. Lachamya is a boy we like. It is a fact that he has been of great help to us in our business. He goes to market and buys pots, jaggery and sal-ammoniac for us. What if he does not belong to us? He has been more helpful to us than our own people. I also wish to give Rukki's hand in marriage to him. This Lachamya is an orphan. He has seven to eight acres of land. What is wrong in choosing him as a groom for Rukki?' The elders were taken aback and sat in silence for a while. A little later, Somalya asked calmly, 'Is this true, Lachamya?'

'Yes sir,' Lachamya responded.

'Marriage is not a simple affair, young man. Do your people accept this proposal? There should be no issues later, you see. Jaga dhekhun, phaga bandhoon kacch (before becoming a groom, it's necessary to be worldly-wise). We should not enter into matrimony in a hurry. Check with your people and discuss things.'

Several appeals to give up did not change the stance taken by Lachamya. Duglibai was also firm in her resolve. The elders spent some time discussing the issue among themselves and later, addressing Lachamya directly, one of the elders asked, 'In that case, the marriage has to be performed according to our rites. You should lead life like our people. Do you agree to abide by these conditions?'

'Who are my relatives? I have no one. Nobody bothers to find out whether I have had my food or not, it matters little to them whether I am alive or dead. I am prepared to marry Rukki. I shall obey all your commands,' said Lachamya.

'What do you say, Rukki?' the elders questioned.

Rukki nodded her head in acceptance.

Finally, Somalya pronounced his decree, 'If an outsider enters the Thanda like a wild bull, we need to worry about it. This young man has agreed to marry Rukki. Duglibai has also consented to it. Besides, Lachamya is in possession of property and fields. Let us all elders consent to it.' Nayak had a generous attitude and wished Rukki a good life while stating his hope that Duglibai would not drag her daughter into her own trade.

Limbya's attempt to prove that the modesty of a local girl had been played with by an outsider had taken a different turn and his anger increased as he lost Rukki in the process as well. 'Limbya has asked the Ghor Panchayat to meet without understanding the problem properly. As a penalty, he has to offer a goat to the panchayat. Duglibai has to distribute liquor among all the elders,' was the final decision arrived at.

Rukki's love affair received adequate publicity because of the stand taken by Somalya and the support given to the couple by the elders. I admired the panchayat system here. But the entire night was filled with noise. When the priest sacrificed a goat and separated its head from its body to make an offering to the god in Mariyamma's temple, I was shocked and thought, 'What sort of people are these!' It was a frightening sight for me, a strict vegetarian. I was feeling disgusted as people were drinking liquor and feasting on meat throughout the night. But I also appreciated the spirit with which they shared food among all, and the pleasure they took in distributing food from house to house, thoroughly enjoying the occasion.

Eight

Dhadi reached the Thanda in the evening with a sling bag and a sarangi hung over his shoulder. He was a tall and pleasant person wearing a yellow turban and a well-groomed moustache. He was a wandering performer who would entertain people with songs woven around the tales of Lambada heroes and other great personalities. I learnt that he was a well-informed artist who constantly moved from place to place visiting various settlements and villages. Since he was new to me, I gathered as much information about him as I could. I also learnt that he was going to narrate the story of Sevalal in the evening. His narration gave me an opportunity to know more about Sevalal who had so far been merely a name. It was a godsend chance to satisfy my curiosity about Sevalal, who was an integral part of the lives of the people here.

Dhadi went directly to Somalya's house and was received with respect and hospitality. Dahilya, the messenger, was sent round the Thanda to announce the event. People, with children in tow, started arriving at the platform under the neem tree after dinner, armed with quilts and rugs. Dhadi began the narration in his own style to the accompaniment of the sarangi.

jai jai karthar baba sevalal
bhima dharminiro pet, jalmeri avathaari
sevalal brahmachari, kaladhari

ramer avathari, chado ghode par savari
sharan ayejeer rakshakar, bhandar bharpurkar
serema savva ser kar.

Son of Bhim and Dharminibai;
Celibate and generous you are
Rider of a white horse, Ram incarnate
Protect us; we seek refuge in you,
Fill the granaries of our Thanda
Help us reap benefits forever and ever.
Ward off the evil, drive away the darkness
Of ignorance, and lend us light.
May your protection reach out to all Lambadas
Be with your tribe of Gora Banjara
And forever protect us.

'Baba Sevalal, we have taken refuge in you. Protect those who seek refuge. Fill the granaries of the Thanda to the full. Bless us that our wealth and prosperity increases manifold.' As Dhadi offered his prayer, full of devotion, with his eyes closed, Somalya also closed his eyes and joined his hands in reverence without moving from where he was seated. Somalya appeared to be completely steeped in meditation. People were eager to listen to the story with their eyes and ears open.

'The practice of celebrating the festival in honour of Sevalal with grandeur on Ramanavami continues to this day in Pourgad of Akola district in Maharashtra. It is a sacred place of pilgrimage for our people. This great man was born in a thanda near Mangalore in Gutti, Bellary district. In that thanda lived a couple – Bhimanayak and Dharminibai. True to their name, they were really dharmathmas (religious and pious souls). But what a pity, though forty years had passed since their marriage, they did not have any children. Dharminibai had to bear the disgrace of being called a barren woman. She offered her prayers to all the gods, undertook vows and visited many temples. Her suffering was

unbearable. Bhimanayak was also worried about the continuation of his progeny. He lost a lot of weight and became very thin. He began a penance. It was a fierce penance. He continued the penance for twelve long years without caring for sun, rain, wind or cold. In heaven, all the seven gods were discussing the need for a faithful servant of the gods to be born on this earth. They thought, "Bhimanayak is performing a rigorous penance; we shall bless him on condition that his first born be devoted to our service."

'Mariyamma makes her presence evident to Bhimanayak and asks him – what does she say? She says, "I am pleased with your penance. Son, ask for a boon; ask whatever you wish for."

– "Mother, bless me with children."

– "Not one, I will bless you with four children. But your first born should be named Seva, and should be devoted to my service after he attains the age of twelve."

– "As you wish, mother," he said.

– "Thathastu."

'Days passed. Dharminibai conceived. The husband and wife continued their prayers. As they were engaged in these prayers, she completed the full term of pregnancy – nine months and nine days.

'Sevalal was born of her sacred womb. There was light. The house was filled with bright light. Mother and father were extremely happy! He glittered like the sun rising in the east. There was laughter in the house. There was chirping of the birds in the trees outside the house. As time passed, they had three more children. They were named Haapa, Baddu and Bana.

'You know, our people do not stay in one place. They move from place to place in search of fodder for their cattle or out of fear that something untoward may happen. So Bhimanayak left Gutti, Bellary, and where did he go? He reached Sirasgad. It is called Sirsi today. Sevalal was a small boy then. He went with boys of his age group, Sakya and Patya, to graze cattle.

His mother, Dharminibai, used to pack lunch for her beloved son. She advised him, "Son, don't go hungry for long, open the pack and eat your lunch." But he never opened his lunch pack. Do you wonder what he did? He gave away his packed lunch to his companions. He fed them to their satisfaction and went to the banks of the stream and made puris and halwa out of sand and ate that. And what else did he do? He made drums out of boulders, made cymbals out of dry leaves and sang bhajans (devotional songs). This is how Sevalal's childhood began, with some miracles – what next?

'Bhimanayak moved from Sirasgad to Nizamabad and from there to Hyderabad city. He got the job of supplying food and ammunition to the soldiers in Nizam's army. Later, he settled down in Ruyigada district of Maharashtra. Bhimanayak was drowned in happiness learning about the miracles of his son. In the meantime, the boy attained twelve years of age. Nayak began to worry. "How can I live without this boy? What do I do if the goddess asks me for him?" As was destined, the goddess did come and ask for him. "Send your son into my service. He is now twelve years old," she reminded him. He told her, "As you wish mother. You ask him and take him with you." The boy then says, "How can I serve you without serving my aged mother and father? It is better to serve my parents than serve you." Mariyamma seethed with anger at his reply. Her eyes were red like burning embers. In spite of that, Sevalal stood his ground and repeated what he had said. It was then that Sevalal began to suffer the effects of Mariyamma's wrath. What all did she do? What all did she do? She took away the life of his younger brother, Bana. She destroyed his cattle. She destroyed all the grain stored in the granary and rendered utter poverty upon them. Alas! They suffered a lot. Poverty is a bad thing. How many troubles did she thrust upon them? One, two, innumerable. He began to sell grass (fodder) to feed his family. She made sure that he did not get any grass. Once, he was able to find some grass. He was engaged in cutting it. But she made him cut his own finger. The blood spurted out like a fountain. But he did not lose his courage. That was the commitment, the commitment of Sevalal. But the goddess was adamant; she had made up her mind to make him a sacrificial animal. Wonder! She was ready to grab him with her mouth wide open – within which all the seven worlds were seen – and tongue outstretched, assuming the form of the universe, with the sun and the moon as her eyes. At that point, Sevalal surrendered to the power of the goddess Mariyamma and agreed to serve her. But he did not agree without his own conditions. What were his conditions? He made a deal with the goddess. She should bring his brother Bana back to life and restore the lost cattle and all the wealth to his parents. Also, "Anything I say should become real," he said. "Thathastu," said the goddess.

'Sevalal began to serve Mariyamma with devotion. He was also helping people and considered it as equal to serving the goddess. People began to praise him. They praised him wholeheartedly. But some people teased him without understanding his powers. Once, his uncle Narsingh Dada Ramavath dressed his son Chingarya as a girl, and asked him to prostrate before Sevalal, seeking from him blessings to beget a child. "Okay, I have granted your wish," said Sevalal. Chingarya was transformed into a girl. Being blessed by Sevalal, he gave birth to a child.

'Miracles like this happen. Zuri, a jeweller from Mumbai, traded in pearls and diamonds. His ship, sailing across the Indian Ocean laden with pearls and diamonds, was caught in a storm. A terrible storm! The hurricane seemed to seal earth and heaven together. He began to wail, "Alas, what is the fate of my ship?" He offered his prayers to all the gods. But it was in vain. Then somebody asked him to seek Sevalal's blessings. He prayed to Sevalal. His ship was rescued from the storm. He offered a huge amount of wealth as gift to Sevalal. There are several such miracles.

'Sevalal's fame spread far and wide. All the Lambadas began

to worship Sevalal instead of Mariyamma. How did Mariyamma take this? She was someone given to temper tantrums. She wanted to take revenge for she had to face embarrassment and humiliation because of him. The fire of her revenge was burning bright, fiercer than the fire in a stove, a fire that would not spare anything, small or big. One needs to be extra strong to escape such fire. One needs strong will. Mariyamma was determined to destroy Sevalal's power and influence. She hatched a plan to ruin him. "If he got married and lost his celibacy," she thought, "his power would automatically be destroyed." She summoned Sevalal and gently counselled him, "My son, you should get married; beget children and see that your clan continues!"

"Impossible!" was his determined response. "I am a brother to all the womenfolk in this world. Therefore, I cannot get married," he argued.

"I shall get you a girl from the other world," countered Mariyamma. Sevalal did not concede to that suggestion either. Where did this argument take them? A case that is not decided in the lower court is taken to the higher court, isn't it? This was not a case to be decided in this world. Therefore, both of them had to go to heaven to the Lord himself.

'Sevalal went to heaven. Can you imagine how he went? Listen, listen to me carefully. In preparation for his journey, he summoned his brothers and gathered a lot of neem leaves. Yes, he asked them to fetch neem leaves. He lay down on a bed of neem leaves and said – what did he say? – he said, "Until I get up all by myself, nobody should touch me. Until I return, lamps should be lit in four corners of this bed and they should never be put out; there should be bhajans sung constantly, and nobody should inform my mother."

'Having given such instructions, he covered himself entirely with more leaves and fell asleep on his bed of neem leaves. There was incense burning all around, issuing forth thick, fragrant smoke. He started ascending higher and higher – All of you, cheer Sevalal! Jai Sevalal! Jai Sevabhai! – Mariyamma and Sevalal presented their cases to the Lord. Having listened to both sides of the case, the Lord gave his grand judgement. "Sevalal is a strict disciplinarian and celibate. Let him be as he is." Sevalal was ecstatic. He had argued in the court of Lord Shiva and came out victorious. But the goddess felt humiliated. She could not tolerate it. She somehow wanted to take revenge and started plotting against him. The harm that comes from scheming, jealousy and revenge need not be explicitly mentioned by me. Mariyamma descended to earth swiftly. She disguised herself as a koravanji (wandering mendicant woman and a soothsayer) and went to Dharminibai and told her, "It has been three days since your son breathed his last." The mother's heart was broken. She ran to the place where Sevalal's body was kept, wailing loudly, filled with great sorrow. This was how Mariyamma deceived Dharminibai. All of you know how many types of deceit there are. Poor woman, she went there hurriedly believing that her son was really dead. All efforts by Haapa, Baddu and Bana to stop her failed. She fell on the body of Sevalal, crying loudly and uncontrollably. Something that should not have happened had happened. Sevalal's body rose from the ground and fell back to the ground, bouncing three times. Life escaped the mortal body. Sevalal gave up his mortal body in Pouragad of Maharashtra. When his body was cremated with neem wood and ghee, from the raging fire arose a voice assuring everyone gathered there, "Saath peedimayi avatar leeyu – I shall be born again after seven generations."

'After a lapse of twelve years, Sevabhai issued a divine message. All of you listen to it with rapt attention. "Gorabhai, there is no need for any of you to be upset. Build a settlement a couple of miles away from the village. Don't visit doctors. The herbs in the forest will protect you. If you consume a pinch of ash from my cremation, you will be rid of all ailments." Since then, Sevabhai has been protecting all of us. Sevabhai has become a god like Mariyamma for all of us. We have hoisted flags in front of both the temples. If a red flag flutters in front of the temple of the goddess, a white flag flies in front of Sevalal's temple. With these two flags flying, epidemics like cholera and plague will be frightened to linger around us.

'Do you know who Sevabhai and Mariyamma are? They are not outsiders. They are all within each one of us. Every human being has two life forces within. One force has elements such as wisdom, generosity, sacrifice – this is called the satvika force. The other force is the tamasa force. Mariyamma is the representative of the tamasa force. Sevabhai is the satvika force. There has always been a conflict between these forces both within and outside us. Let us remember the ascetic Sevabhai with devotion.

satya seva bhaya, sadguru chhaya
bala karunalu chhaya
namma nuvu apathu dooramadi
kala kattaladaga jyothiyagi
kai hididu nadesu chhaya   (1)

ba ba chhayaga sharanu maadona
jai jai sevalal annona

satya guru, satya guru sevalal baapu
thona namaskar, thona namaskar.   (2)

The shadow of sadguru has spread
In the form of truth and goodness
The shadow that is kind and gentle
Driving away the evil forces from us
Becoming a guiding lamp in darkness
Lead us by hand, Oh Lord.

Come let us offer our salutations to the Lord
Let's hail Sevalal
Satya guru, Satya guru, Sevalal Baapu
Our salutations, our salutations to you.

'The shout of "Jai Sevalal" received a resounding response by all.

'Let us say "Jai" to Mariyamma also. Let us ask her to grant us our wish. "Mother, don't trouble us, don't let us develop tamasa forces," prayed Dhadi. All the people cheered once again. They were devoted to Mariyamma out of a sense of fear, while they were devoted to Sevalal out of love for his compassion, service, and generosity.'

The people gathered there started going back to their homes, ruminating about the songs and the story narrated by Dhadi. While preparing to retire for the night in a corner of the platform, Dhadi informed Somalya of a groom in Ghatagi Thanda for his daughter. He mentioned that though it was a second alliance for the groom, he was well-to-do, with several heads of cattle in his possession. He finally said, 'If the proposal is acceptable to you, I shall fetch the groom and his elders for negotiation in a few days.' Somalya, who was pleased with the narration, appeared doubly pleased with this information.

I was disappointed. Dhadi had projected himself as an artist while narrating the story, a philosopher interpreting the deeper layers of meaning. Immersed in his devotion, with closed eyes, during the performance he had appeared as a veritable messenger of Sevalal. But now, he appeared to be a broker who solicits parties for money, and a cruel hunter who appeared on the scene to destroy the life of the sprightly, young, deer-like Zimri. What a groom was chosen for Zimri! I can empathize with people who have given birth to daughters. I have the responsibility of finding a groom for my younger sister. Are there any parents who do not wish their daughters to be happy? But how can we look for financial prosperity alone as a deciding factor? Though it was a matter restricted to Somalya's family, I could not help feeling depressed as I left the place.

As the image of a speeding deer being chased by a hunter was fading from my mind, I began to recall Dhadi's intense narration of the conflict between the hero Sevalal and Mariyamma.

Nine

Though the people of the Thanda were unhappy with the judgement given by Somalya Nayak in the case of Limbya, it had had different consequences in Kalluru. Lachamya's uncle, Yenkappa, wanted to give his daughter in marriage to him. He wanted to appropriate his wealth through this marriage. As soon as he heard the news of a marriage proposal from the Thanda for Lachamya, he hurriedly came to Kalluru. He wove a spicy story, telling everyone that the Lambadas proposed to give their girl in marriage to Lachamya and convert him into a Lambada. He spread this story among the people of the village.

He went round the village, met all the elders, and convinced them that though there are many factions and internal squabbles in the village, all of them should unite as one in their fight against the Thanda in this matter. He implied, 'If we encourage the people of the Thanda like this, tomorrow they will swallow us. This is a warning bell to caution us to be careful.' The village elders believed him and agreed with his views on the matter. Some thought of inviting Somalya Nayak for a discussion, whereas others felt it was best to counsel Lachamya and send him with Yenkappa to his village.

Yenkappa summoned a few elders to counsel his nephew. One of the elders made Lachamya sit next to him and in a very affectionate tone began to tell him, 'Our relationship with such people should be casual; we should visit them in the late evenings and return at dawn, nothing beyond that. What a fool you are to carry this relationship through to marriage? You have agreed to this marriage perhaps in a state of emotional attachment or under some pressure exerted by them. Tomorrow when you beget children, a bigger problem will arise. How can you survive as a Lambada? Think it over. Don't succumb under pressure and lose your ability to think calmly. There are many such among us, Chandri the scavenger, Renuka the cobbler, Pinjar Bibi the Muslim – relationships with such people should be like having snacks at a tea shop. It is different from having a meal at home; the relationships should be as casual. Think well, don't be in a hurry.' Another person added, 'Marry Yenkappa's daughter. The old relationships are another matter. You will be happy. Look here, just don't step into the Thanda at all. We thought you were going there casually. We did not know that your visits would come to this. These people are dangerous. They are after your house and fields. Besides, that Limbya is coveting the girl, and if he harms you what will be your fate? Don't lose your life for a hasty decision. Limbya can be ruthless.'

Lachamya began to understand the intention hidden in these suggestions. The fears he had nursed within himself were being expressed by these elders. After this incident, Lachamya never went anywhere near the Thanda. Yenkappa arranged the marriage of his daughter with Lachamya post haste and took him to his village after selling the house and lands that belonged to him.

In the Thanda, Rukki began to weep and moan. There was no chance of Lachamya coming back to the Thanda. Duglibai was not affected the way Rukki was. She had decided that there was only one way left open for her. But Rukki did not want to take the path shown by her mother.

The villagers decided not to let the matter rest; they wanted revenge. The elders of the village thought, 'These Lambadas who work on our farms as labourers are conspiring to make one of our boys become part of their community! What arrogance!' They invited Somalya Nayak and the elders for a discussion. Somalya Nayak said rather sternly, 'We are not at fault in this matter. You can check with Lachamya. He was with Rukki and both had mutually agreed to the marriage, and this prompted us to help them get married. Please bear in mind, never consider our girls as "use and throw" objects.'

The elders of the village flared up in anger. 'How can people who work as labourers be so arrogant? They work so hard, let them live – was what we thought. But see what they have done to us. We never thought they would stoop to this level,' they murmured among themselves. One of the elders tried to bring matters under control. 'Look here,' he said, 'we will not interfere with your internal matters and how you settle quarrels among your people. But when a boy from the village was involved, was it not appropriate to inform the elders of the village? From now on, will you take up the governance of the village as well? In matters such as this, you should not take any decision without our knowledge. In the first place, you should keep a check on your girls. Instead, you talk irrelevantly. Is that appropriate?' His voice was stern.

After Somalya was sent back, the villagers began to discuss the matter among themselves, and concluded, 'Lambadas work hard, strain their bodies and have begun to prosper. Therefore, they are becoming bold enough to speak to us in this manner.'

After returning to the Thanda, Somalya and the elders summoned Duglibai. Somalya poured out his anguish and despair. 'Look here Duglibai,' he said, 'The village people have humiliated us and sent us back. If we had kept our girls under control and disciplined them, we would not have had to face this humiliation from those people. They have understood our weakness and are looking down at us with contempt. It is true, we are poor, this stomach is evil, it can drive us to do anything, but if we lose our dignity and respect, is it worth living?'

Duglibai's energy was sagging and she did not have as much fire left in her as she had had in the earlier meeting. 'What happened was very different from what I had thought and planned. What can I do?' Duglibai spoke in a repentant tone. 'Rukki has been weeping and moaning for some nights. In the middle of the night, she suddenly bursts into loud shrieks and sits up on her bed. She bangs her forehead against the walls and wails, "I've been cheated, I've been cheated." All words of encouragement I speak are disregarded and she looks at me as if I am her enemy. She stares at me with her eyes wide open. I never imagined she would become like this. What shall I do? Please suggest some remedy for my daughter.' As she spoke, Duglibai started weeping. 'You go now. We will discuss the matter,' said Somalya. Having sent her away, Somalya and the elders began to discuss among themselves.

'We have to save Rukki, otherwise Duglibai will take her into her trade,' said one of the elders.

'Why don't we ask Limbya to marry her?' asked another elder

'Would he agree to it?' Somalya was doubtful.

'Let's see,' said the others and decided to approach Limbya.

In four-five days Limbya got to know about the decision taken by the elders. Rukki also heard of this. Ruplibai went to Duglibai's hut and in the course of their conversation, broached the topic. Rukki began to weep. 'Take heart. Think of your future. Whatever had to happen, has happened. There's no point crying over it. You will not get back the past. Tell us what you want to do now,' said Ruplibai.

'I was fascinated by Lachamya's glamour. I never knew he would leave me in deep waters,' said Rukki.

'He might have left you in deep waters, but you must not drown; you should swim, you should win,' said Ruplibai. After much persuasion, Rukki consented to marry Limbya, if he was willing.

❖

On the other side of the Thanda, Kasanu was counselling Limbya in a similar manner. 'What had to happen has happened. We never knew the village boy and his people would deceive us in this manner. We are also at fault. Rukki has also made mistakes. Anyhow, what you desired is likely to happen now. Take a generous view and agree to the marriage. You can give life to her.' In response, Limbya said, 'I will abide by the decision of the elders.'

The elders were called for the final meeting of the panchayat. Rukki and Limbya were also called by the elders to the Panchayat platform. One of the elders initiated the discussion by asking Rukki directly, 'If you want to get settled in life, you have to marry Limbya; what do you say to this?' Rukki, who was crying incessantly, replied rather haltingly, 'When he proposed to me, I rejected him. How can I shamelessly ask him to marry me now?' Another of the elders said, 'We will ask him. If he consents, will you agree?' She nodded her head in affirmation. Limbya agreed to the marriage and earned praises from everyone. Limbya grew in stature in the eyes of all the people of the thanda. Rukki's eyes were filled with tears at the thought of getting support from Limbya and her life finding a new direction.

Ten

When I went to Nagarkote to draw my salary I met a teacher who belonged to the Lambada community and made friends with him. Having learnt about my interest in the Thanda, he took me to the president of the Banjara Association. He gathered all the details of the difficulties existing in the Thanda and promised to visit it some time. His name was Hiralal, and he was a labour leader in the Nagarkote Cotton Mills. It was evident from his manner of speaking that he was smart.

There were some three or four youngsters in the Thanda who had attended school or college and were partially educated. Somalya's son Hari alone had passed the board examinations and continued his education in a college. His second son, Loku, Kasanu's son, Dhenya and Khubya's son, Dooda could not clear the pre-university course and had bid goodbye to college education. These boys would gather in Mariyamma's temple when the elders were not around and spend time gossiping or playing cards.

Since I had requested, they all began to come to school. I suggested that we get electricity to the Thanda, lay a road between the Thanda and Kalluru and introduce a bus service connecting the two places. But they said they needed jobs before taking up this work. 'If you are determined, you can find jobs here itself,' I said.

'How?'

'Look at the grazing grounds. It is a piece of land with plenty of water.'

'But there are too many stones. No matter how much you dig, only stones come out,' said one of them.

'There will be stones inside the earth; that is natural. Are we planting trees? The soil here is good enough for growing crops. We can grow paddy; in case of water shortage, we may grow jowar and millets.' I also told them about my meeting with Hiralal, the president of the Banjara Association and mentioned his efforts to have these lands awarded to the Thanda.

In the evening, when all the elders had gathered, I brought up this topic again. The elders and the youth accepted the proposal. I felt satisfied.

There was some progress on the school front. Children had started coming to the school in a well-groomed manner. Zimri had learnt to read and write. She showed interest in reading adventure stories. I used to provide her with books she might enjoy.

❖

Somalya turned his attention to his daughter Zimri once the matter of Rukki's marriage had been settled. Loku had made enquiries about the rich groom suggested by Dhadi and gathered that he was a middle-aged man with three children and a dead wife. A serious discussion took place between Ruplibai and Somalya. Ruplibai, who had intentions of marrying her daughter into her parents' family, argued, 'However prosperous a groom may be, can we choose an old man for our daughter?' In response, Somalya said, 'Is there a possibility of finding rich grooms among us? He is said to have several herds of sheep and goat and cows and oxen. He has irrigated lands. Let us give her away to him. The girl will be happy. After all, girls grow old after giving birth to a couple of children. How will the difference in age matter?' Even when the entire household stood against him, Somalya did not give up his stand. 'The daughter will have plenty to eat and drink and will be happy, don't you understand?' he scolded. Next day, Zimri came to school earlier than usual with a sad face and started sweeping the room. Her eyes filled with tears when I spoke to her. When I asked her what had happened, she narrated the entire episode to me.

'Why don't you frankly tell your father what is on your mind?' I asked her. 'Who will listen to me?' she replied. I consoled her saying, 'I will talk to your father, don't be disheartened.'

Zimri came back with her mother in the afternoon. I was surprised. I greeted her by saying, 'Welcome, come in please.' Zimri hid behind her mother, cracking her knuckles and drawing designs in the mud with her big toe. Ruplibai patiently narrated all that had passed about her daughter's marriage and requested me to intervene in the matter. Giving assurance to her I said, 'I shall at a proper time broach the topic with your husband and try to convince him.'

'I need another help. You usually go to Nagarkote to draw your salary. Get a blouse stitched for Zimri. My brother has bought a sari for Zimri. Take one of her blouses with you, for measurements. I take this liberty for I consider you as one among us.'

'It's all right. I shall get it stitched,' I said. I agreed to this as I did not want to disappoint either the girl or her mother.

When Zimri was alone, I handed over the blouse I had got stitched for her, concealed in a book. Her eyes shone with gratitude.

I had not yet broached the topic of her marriage with her father. One evening, when I wanted to discuss the topic, he seemed a little disturbed. But since the matter had been postponed long enough, I said, 'Look for a good groom for Zimri. Why are you obsessed with the idea of property and prosperity?'

'Master, please don't interfere in every matter,' he retorted.

I was shocked. I realized I was unnecessarily getting involved in matters that didn't concern me. For a couple of minutes both of us sat in silence. A little later, Somalya began, 'Who asked you to get the blouse stitched? When the innocent women asked you for a favour, you should have refused. Otherwise, you could have informed me. Instead, you got the blouse stitched. When my daughter wore the blouse, I came to know what had happened.'

'As I was considered a member of the family, I had to oblige. Nothing more to it,' I explained.

'We are not prepared to do away with our traditions and practices. These women are senseless; can sari and blouse be grander than our traditional dress of the skirt, blouse and the veil? Should we become completely like you? If we have to progress, we don't need to give up what is ours. Today, our traditional trades are dying out; we are not prepared for this setback to our religion and culture. If my religion is hurt, I cannot tolerate it. We tried to prevent Rukki's affair. The villagers in turn wanted to teach us a lesson. What can we do? We had no option but to apologize to them. We may depend on them for work, but we are not prepared to sell ourselves to them.' Somalya spoke with great emotion. He was not prepared to listen to me at any cost.

Somalya did not come to school for the next two or three days. I felt bad. Zimri was also not sent to school.

Several days passed. It was not clear whether her uncle came and took her away or whether Zimri ran away with him voluntarily. The news somehow reached me. Somalya was enraged. He stopped communicating with his wife and son as he understood that they had encouraged Zimri, against his wishes.

Somalya went in search of his daughter with his friend Kasanu. He went to his in-law's place and roughed up his aged parents-in-law. 'He said he would go to Goa in search of a job, and beyond that, we know nothing,' said his father-in-law. On their way home, Somalya and Kasanu met someone else, who confirmed that Zimri and her uncle had gone to Goa.

For a few days after returning to the Thanda, Somalya did not seem to go to work. Morning and evening, he would be found in the Sevalal temple, singing bhajans to the accompaniment of a tambura. Otherwise, he would keep striking the cymbals. Loku came to me and requested, 'Father has been behaving strangely, please talk to him, master.'

'He misunderstood me earlier. Why do I need to involve myself in unnecessary things? Please let me be,' I said.

'No master, he has a good opinion of you. He does not even listen to Kasanu uncle. To avoid her being married off to an old man, I have myself sent Zimri away with uncle. Please make my father understand,' he pleaded.

'Let me see,' I said.

Somalya, who seemed to be avoiding me all these days, came to the school one day. 'You must try to forget all this. Wherever she may be, wish your daughter well. Wish for her happiness,' I said.

'It is easy to say that. I doted on my daughter. She should not have done this to me. I am the one who dispenses justice in the Thanda. How can my own daughter run away like this? It's all right; I'll consider her dead, banished from my life. Master, was it a mistake to send her to school?' he asked.

'Don't think her going to school has anything to do with her leaving home. You tried to impose your views on her against her wishes. It is true, that one needs money and comfort. But more important than that is love; you forgot that,' I blurted out.

After this conversation, there was not a single day when Somalya did not meet me; he would at least exchange a few words with me every day. 'Please do not misunderstand me, master. I had spoken out of anger,' he said. 'Please get in touch with the president of the Banjara Association. Let us know the legal position about the grazing grounds. We shall all discuss the matter,' he said, emphatically. I said I would write a letter to him.

Eleven

Damla, who had mysteriously disappeared from the Thanda, came back. But I was surprised when he did not come to the school. I asked his son what had happened. 'He is down with fever,' he informed me.

A few days later, all of a sudden, I got a message from him through his son, asking me to go and see him at his house. I was in two minds about whether or not to go, but finally, I started walking towards his house after school hours. His hut was tiny, like a sparrow's nest. I wondered how the well-built Damla could live in this hut. The thought of the giant Damla crouched in his tiny hut filled me with compassion. The house was full of children and aged parents. It was then that I realized the reason he had converted the school premises into his lodgings. His father was sleeping outside in the yard wrapped in a quilt, while his mother was curled up in a corner, shivering. A goat was bleating next to Damla's bed where he lay, moaning, 'Ha...Ham, it's paining, oh god!' His wife was giving him fomentation from a hot griddle.

As soon as I entered the hut, Damla's wife hurriedly spread something on the floor for me to sit on. As I sat, Damla tried to get up, but he was unable to do so. A dog came into the hut from outside and climbed on his bed. Children were crying and calling for attention. It was a stuffy and suffocating place. I was being bitten by ticks and bugs. I felt like getting out of that hut as soon as possible.

'There is nothing to hide from you,' began Damla as I sat next to him. 'The police arrested me and beat me so much that I cannot get up. My elbows and knees are gone. They stuffed my eyes and anus with chilli powder and beat me. Oh, god! Don't pass on my trade to my children, let this end with me! Teach them a few letters and give them life. I need to feed the old mother, father, children and others. I can't give up this habit of drinking. Over and above this, I need to eat meat every alternate day. In this way...'

'Let it be. Don't worry about unnecessary things now, get well first; don't strain yourself by talking too much,' I said, trying to console him.

'Give me five rupees. I shall return it after I sell this goat,' he said. I knew he would ask me for money. Since he needed money badly, I did not bargain this time and gave him five rupees and got out of there, saying, 'Recover speedily.'

Damla had lost most of his pride and arrogance of earlier days. He was not noisy as he would earlier be when intoxicated. He seemed to have been tamed.

Later I got to know more about him. He was well known as a thief who would steal sheep. He would join two other friends from other settlements, enter the barns, steal sheep, kill them and feast on the meat. Those who came in search of lost sheep would not find them. He would eat to his fill and sleep soundly. But the shepherds had always suspected him to be the thief. Once, he and his friends were sleeping soundly after a heavy meal. There were some pieces of meat left in a vessel on the stove. The shepherds brought the police with them, who had been informed of the theft well in advance. Damla's friends woke up with a start and began to run, but were caught by the police. Damla, however, had to be woken up by having his sides poked with a baton. He woke up shouting, 'Why? Why?'

'You bastard! First, carry this vessel on your head!' ordered the police and marched him away.

As they were walking behind the police, carrying the vessel, the three stealthily took out pieces of meat from the vessel and began eating, finishing the meat inside it. When they sat down to drink water near the stream, they filled the vessel with stones and water on the sly. When they reached the station, the police proudly presented the three, saluted the inspector and said that they had caught the thieves red-handed, with the stolen goods. At that, Damla confidently stated, 'No sir, we are not involved in any theft at all.'

'You bastard, do you lie? Take out the vessel!' roared the policeman.

Damla took the vessel and tipped it over, and all that came out was stones, mud and muddy water. They were scolded and threatened but set free.

When the crops were ready for harvest, Damla would steal ears of jowar, green gram pods and peanuts from the fields. He would bring the stolen goods to his house in the middle of the night for his family to consume, so there would be no trace of it left the next day. He would seek the blessings of Mariyamma before going to steal anything. When he was able to steal more chicken and sheep than he expected, he would sacrifice them to the goddess and share the meat with his neighbours. When he was caught by the police, his wife would sell a sheep or a goat and get him released by using the money to pay for his bail. She also had to pay a penalty to the Thanda panchayat. When the police went to the forest to catch him, they had stones pelted at them. He was capable of throwing nearly ten stones at a time as if they were thrown from different directions. They would feel stones hit them from behind and retreat without bothering him.

People also talked about the time when he went to Aminapur market with eight to ten stolen sheep to sell. The owner informed the police and got him arrested. Several stories and anecdotes about him have become popular.

His wife prayed to Mariyamma for his recovery, and sacrificed to the goddess the only goat that was left. One day, late in the evening, Damla began to shout and rave. The forest guards had arrested five women who had gone to gather firewood in the forest. Among those caught was Damla's wife. When captured, she told the police, 'We know how capable you are! You have caught us who are here to collect firewood for our kitchen, but you let go those who take away logs in trucks. We know you, how you guard, you bastards!' Enraged by this, a guard rushed at her but a woman picked up a piece of wood and hit him on the head. He reeled back and fell down, holding his head in his hands. The guards got angrier at this. They beat them hard on their thighs and bound them with a big rope. They tied up the plait of one woman with that of the other and clapped and laughed aloud when the women tugged at each other, rolling on the ground in an effort to free themselves. Damla went to the hills looking for his wife when she did not return home and found her and her companions bound up and suffering. He set them free and brought them back.

It was on this night that Damla had begun to shout and rave after having his drink. 'I will not spare these bastards who have tortured our women. I will punish them,' he shouted. 'They don't want us to trade liquor, nor cut wood nor collect berries. What are we supposed to do? Should we or should we not survive on this earth? Are we supposed to eat mud? Is this entire earth their fathers' property?' He continued to shout in this manner through the night.

Twelve

Dusk was settling on the Thanda. People who had gone to carry stones to build the road, labourers who had gone to the fields and gardens in Kalluru, fishermen who had gone to catch fish in the lakes and people of all kinds of vocation were returning to the Thanda. Sitting on the platform, I saw a lean man wearing a pyjama and kurta with a sling bag strapped on his shoulder walking down the hillock along with a man who belonged to the Thanda.

As he neared the place, I could make out that he was Hiralal. The person from the Thanda directed him towards me and went his way. He came and joined me at the platform. As I sat there, talking to him, Somalya approached us. He was on his way home when he noticed a stranger sitting with me, and in an effort to recognize him, he had come near us. I introduced Somalya to Hiralal. Somalya was happy, and left saying, 'Please bring him to my house.'

Some odd noise and a few squabbles were usual around the Thanda once everyone returned in the evening. When all such noise subsided, I took Hiralal to Somalya's house. A strange silence pervaded the house due to Zimri's absence. Her sprightly movements and laughter had filled the house with happiness. I wondered how the parents who had brought her up with so much love could take this. Though he appeared stern and full of resolve, I was sure, in his heart of hearts, Somalya was very sad.

As we entered the house, Loku greeted us, spread a mat for us to sit on and left saying, 'Please be seated, father will join you.' In a little while, Somalya came in, wiping his face with a towel, and sat in front of us and started making conversation. Soon, Loku also came and joined us.

I saw Ruplibai at the door holding a tray with cups of tea. Finding a stranger in my company, she stood near the door and called Loku. Loku fetched the tea. She did not look tired and worn out in spite of having worked all through the day. I have never seen her getting upset or depressed at any time. She would always be smiling, with the brightness of moonlight in her smile. Though she was past her prime, she still looked fit and young. She continued to stand at the door after handing over the tea.

Sipping on his tea, Hiralal asked Somalya to assemble people at a place. He said, 'We will make efforts to have the grazing grounds given to you in accordance with the law. We need support from every one of you. In the first place, you should take courage and start cultivating these fields before the issue is taken up legally.' Loku promised to get all his friends to the platform and left.

'Our traditional trades are gradually dying out. If we get these fields, our people will have some means of earning a livelihood. Please see that this work is done at the earliest,' requested Ruplibai from the door. 'We will all put our heads together. Get the womenfolk as well.' So saying, Hiralal got up.

It took a little while for people to assemble as they were persuading each other to come and join the group. Somalya had two lanterns fixed on the platform. Hiralal pleaded with the people to get together to cultivate the grazing grounds. He made room for an open discussion so that a consensus decision could be reached. Seated on the platform were Somalya, the elders, the secretary and Hiralal. They requested me to occupy a seat alongside them.

People began to gather in the open space. They arrived in

singles, pairs, threesomes and small groups. The hugely built Damla arrived twirling his moustache as usual and trying in vain to drive away the dog that followed him. His dog was with him, wagging its tail, when he sat down. Limbya came along with his fellow workers and Loku with his friends. They were in a lighter mood as they came and joined the group. Ruplibai, Duglibai, Rukku, Chandri, Gowri, Lalibai and others came and sat on one side. The priest of Mariyamma temple, who arrived late, was invited to join the others on the platform. The assembly began with an address by Somalya. 'Hiralal, the president of the Banjara Association, Nagarkote taluka, is with us. By now, you are probably aware of the reason for our assembly today. All of us desire to have our own fields and engage in farming. We have assembled here to discuss the consequences of cultivating the grazing grounds that are lying idle.' This was greeted with a loud murmur leading to noisy arguments among the people assembled.

Hiralal stood up and said, 'Please say what you want to say loudly, one after the other. Don't hesitate to put forth your views.' Damla began to speak, twirling his moustache. 'I'll speak frankly. We have been engaged in various trades. Some are engaged as labourers while some are involved in illicit distillation. We sell firewood, fruit and vegetables, and people like me are involved in thieving. Almost all these trades are on the decline. Thus, let's all determine to cultivate the grazing grounds. Mr Hiralal is here to support us. To tell you the truth, I had never thought of this before. Let us now start our work without second thoughts.' Limbya, Loku and the other youngsters clapped in appreciation of what Damla said.

Dhulya seemed to have a contrary view. He warned, 'So far, we have maintained a cordial relation with the people of Kalluru. If we start cultivating the grazing grounds, there may be some problems. Besides, we work in their fields and gardens as labourers. It may be difficult to survive by opposing the people of the village.' Some people said 'yes, yes' in agreement.

At this point, Limbya got up and said emphatically, 'What is more important? Guarding the feelings of the village people or acquiring fields for the Thanda?' Most of the people gathered shouted, 'Fields, fields.'

The leader of the labourers, Hiralal, began his speech in a tone of authority, 'In the first place, we need to make an application to the Deputy Commissioner. All of you need to sign the application. How long it may take for this application to yield results is anybody's guess. So, take courage and begin to till the lands. Let's see what happens. Since Independence, the government has been granting several facilities to backward classes. We have to make use of such facilities. We have to become aware of our rights. Let's all work together. I've prepared an application on your behalf. I will read it to you, please listen.

> *Hon. District Collector,*
>
> *We, the people of Havan Thanda, adjacent to Kalluru village in Nagarkote Taluka wish to appeal to you and bring to your kind notice that there is a three-hundred acre grazing ground next to our Thanda. Since the cattle of Kalluru graze in the hills, this land is not useful to them. If the government can allot this land to us, the nomadic, landless Lambadas, you shall be providing us with a means to live.*
>
> *We humbly appeal to your kind self to have this land allotted to us at the earliest.*
>
> *Yours faithfully,*

All of you need to sign this application. Don't you all agree to sign this?'

Every one shouted 'yes, yes' in response to his call. 'Those who can sign, please sign, others may put their thumb impression,' suggested Hiralal. Somalya, Kasanu and a few educated young people came forward to sign, while Damla, Ramji, Khubya and

Dhulya left their thumb impressions. Duglibai, Ruplibai and other women came forward to express their consent. Duglibai held Hiralal's hand and said, 'You have come here like Sevalal, don't let us down.' She pressed her thumb on the inking pad and left her thumb impression on the paper.

'All of you have been courageous. I will fight with your cooperation. Whatever obstacles come in our way, let's face them together,' said Hiralal.

After our meal, I took Hiralal to the school. He continued to talk about the future course of action. He was concerned about his people. Being a labour leader, he had contacts with several officials and politicians and was evidently street smart. Later, he said that he wanted to leave early in the morning and went to bed and soon started snoring.

As I rolled out the carpet and pulled out the trunk to use it as my pillow, a letter written by my friend Patil caught my attention. I read it again.

Try all means possible and get a transfer out of the Thanda at the earliest. Your parents have also expressed this opinion and asked me to convey this message to you. It is not right for you to stick around there and ruin your life. Is it not really a torture to have to teach those young kids? You must be feeling very lonely and unhappy there...

The letter continued in this way with many more details. I made a note in my diary to respond thus:

I have come to the Thanda with a determination to work and I have challenged myself to do well here! In the beginning, it was difficult to adjust to the new environment. The feeling of loneliness bothered me as I was away from home. I was initially disgusted to see the thieves and drunkards like Damla and the dirty and unkempt children. I often wondered how I would teach these children who were stinking. I was scared at the sight of goats and cocks being sacrificed during festivals, the assemblage of the panchayat or offerings made to Mariyamma. There is no end to the superstitions and traditional beliefs of these people. It is only now that I am adjusting to this world – the love and affection received from Somalya and his family, his eagerness to have the lands cultivated, my tacit support to him in his efforts, the improved attendance of the children at school. Since I have involved myself in all these activities, I am not feeling left out and lonely. This is a new world. I am adjusting to new experiences in the new world. The art and culture exhibited by this neglected group of people is in no way inferior. Somalya is a person committed to the welfare of the people. All the same, he has some idiosyncrasies. When I feel bored, I go to Nagarkote and watch a movie. I have begun to understand the flora and fauna of the place and hold conversation with plants and trees, ponds, streams and hillocks around. It is not possible for me to pen down every experience of mine here in this letter. That is a long story.

I went out to ease myself. I came back, bolted the door and pulled a sheet over myself, but sleep eluded me for a long time.

Thirteen

The people of the Thanda began their work on the grazing grounds the very next morning. Some got busy moving the huge boulders and rocks, some engaged themselves in clearing the thorny bushes and others destroyed the anthills. Khubya said, 'We also need to repair the lake. How can water in this small pond suffice for such a large piece of land?'

'Yes, let's dredge it. Let's also make it a little bigger,' Somalya suggested.

'Let those who have committed themselves to work as labourers go to work. Let some people also practise their trades to earn their living. But let there be at least two or three well-bodied people from each household to work here, that will suffice.' This opinion, expressed by Damla, was endorsed by everyone.

'We agree with you, Damla,' interrupted Emjee, 'but how can we share this land among us in the future?'

'You are someone who stitches clothes for the unborn child,' was Damla's quick response. When Kasanu, Somalya, Khubya and Khemli discussed this among themselves in low, hushed tones, they realized this matter would come up for discussion sometime in the future. Somalya said, 'Let's all work together for a few years. We will harvest the crops and share them among ourselves; let's see how it works out. We may pick lots and share the lands among ourselves later.' Everyone agreed to this suggestion.

Everyone was motivated to work on the land and this was evident in their singing and joking with each other as they engaged themselves in preparing the land for cultivation. In the evening, all of them gathered around the platform and started planning next day's work. The work on the lake took precedence over other matters. The priest said, 'We should worship the lake, make offerings to Mariyamma and then take up the work of dredging.' Ramji, a senior member of the village who was eager to know about the recent happenings in the Thanda arrived at the platform with the help of his huge walking stick. He agreed with the priest, sighed and added, 'Yes, there could be obstacles. I am reminded of the story of our leader and the Kodidharaja Lake.'

'What is it?' everyone assembled seemed curious.

'Long ago, there was a settlement similar to ours. The leader of that settlement was Kodidharaja. He thought the settlement needed a lake. He gathered around twelve thousand people from more than ten villages and started building the embankment. The lake was ready, but there was not a drop of water in it. Without the knowledge of the villagers, a fierce monster would come and drink all the water in the lake and disappear. The lake cried for water. All the elders gathered and asked the priest "Why does this happen?" The priest, with his exceptional insight, revealed that it was a monster's doing. "What is the solution?" asked the elders. Then the priest, possessed by mother Mariyamma, prophesied, "If you sacrifice your son and daughter-in-law to the lake, it will fill with water. The monster will stop drinking the water once he eats the sacrificial humans and heaves a satiated belch."

The Raja was devastated and said, "God, what shall I do now?" Upon learning the reason for his sadness, his son and daughter-in-law said, "We will be glad to sacrifice ourselves if the world can live happily. We will consider ourselves as fortunate to be able to make this sacrifice." So saying, they got ready for the sacrificial ceremony. The huge monster who pervaded the heavens and the earth appeared, roaring, "A new scent, a new scent!" The earth and heaven shook at that instance. Raja's son and daughter-in-law stood by the lake, praying to the almighty goddess. Using the five weapons he had brought with him, Raja's son killed the monster. At that very instance, water started gushing out from mother earth, as the Ganga flows from the locks of the lord. Everyone watched with joy as water started to fill and subsequently overflow from the lake. Everyone wholeheartedly praised the son of Kodidharaja, calling him Dharmaraja (a character from the Mahabharata, known for his righteousness). Where do we find people who are prepared to make such sacrifices these days? Sacrificing themselves to save the world?'

When Ramji posed this question at the end of his narration, everyone started looking at each other, their eyes wide open. Somalya stood up and said in all seriousness, 'If the lake can get filled by sacrificing someone, I am ready to sacrifice my life. All of us will die some day. If I die for this cause, I may earn some merit in my afterlife.' Ramji interjected, 'Why do you talk of death? Shun it! The sum and substance of all this is that we need to work hard, sacrificing our selfishness to make our Thanda prosperous.' At this moment, the priest who was sitting there began to tremble. 'The goddess has arrived, goddess has arrived, possessing him,' said some people, at once recognizing the symptoms. A loud wail emanated from his mouth. Kasanu asked, 'Mother, how are you? Why have you come now?'

'Listen, children, why is Sevalal's temple in good condition while my temple lies broken? Celebrate my festival and fair without fail.'

'Mother, with your blessings, let the lake get filled with water, let there be crops in the grazing grounds. We shall build your temple and also have a fair,' pleaded Somalya.

'In that case, listen to me. You have to offer sacrifices; sacrifice five cocks to appease me.' Somalya, Ramji and the rest folded their hands in supplication and appealed to the goddess. 'Mother, be at peace. Be kind to us. We shall make the sacrifice as per your wish next Tuesday,' assured an elder member.

Tuesday being an auspicious day devoted to the worship of the goddess, a resolution was passed. 'Nobody should go out of the Thanda that day. We have to give offerings to the goddess. Nobody should cook in their house. Cocks have to be sacrificed.' This was announced across the Thanda. Next Tuesday, everyone, including the children, gathered outside the temple of the goddess. The festival was worth witnessing; the priest performed a special puja, sacrificed a goat, severed its head and placed the head and body separately in front of the idol. My heart sank at the ease with which he severed the goat's head, as if breaking a coconut. Meanwhile, Somalya made an earnest plea to the goddess, 'Are we not non-entities in your presence for you are the mighty one who could put to test Sevalal? Let the lake be filled with Ganga. Mother, don't test us. May your blessing always protect us.' Everyone participated in the celebrations happily. After everyone had had their lunch, the sacrament was sent to each house in the Thanda.

Those who had received education at the school were not interested in celebrations of this kind. But they all looked forward to the sumptuous meal on occasions like this. Everyone had a hearty meal and were happy. Jowar and rice, the grains that were offered to the goddess, reached the priest's house.

Subsequently, the work on the dredging of the lake and clearing of the grazing grounds was attended to at a quick pace. Doodya, Dhenya and Loku, along with some other youngsters, worked with enthusiasm. Loku had taken the responsibility of gathering all the young people in the Thanda to work on dredging the lake as well as digging a canal along the bund to carry water to the fields. While Dhenya concentrated on the work assigned, Doodya was critical of Loku, 'This fellow wants to boss over us; he tries to order us around. Bastard!' Dhenya tried to pacify him, saying, 'Let's not try to break our unity; it's necessary to work together. All five fingers cannot be alike, can they be?'

❖

Damla's schedule had been modified. He started working on the fields with his wife and children right from the early hours of the morning. He no longer whiled away his time on the school premises. His wife used to get up early in the morning, cook food and pack lunch before going to work. Damla had been assigned a portion of the land. Everyone had been instructed to till their share of land and keep it ready.

Duglibai curtailed her illicit liquor brewing business. When clients from Kalluru came to her house, she sent them back, telling them that she had given up her trade. The few others in the Thanda who were engaged in the same business restricted their activities to brewing only enough liquor to suffice the needs of the Thanda on occasions such as festivals, weddings or sacrificial offerings. But the raids of the excise personnel and the rounding up and thrashing of the brewers continued. Limbya and Rukki were clearing the grass and weed and talking to each other. While he cut the bushes, she would drag them away and place them in a heap. They were waiting for the day when the elders would decide on a date for their marriage.

The labourers Somalya, Kasanu and Khubya stopped going to Kalluru with their bullocks to work and started tilling the grazing grounds instead. They had to till not only their share of the land, but also the land that belonged to others. Nobody other than these three owned bullocks.

The people of Kalluru started feeling the pinch as the labour supply from the Thanda began to dry up. Hunters, shepherds and lower caste people in the village began working as labourers on the fields. But none were as hardy as the Lambadas. Since they had stopped working, the people of Kalluru started facing problems. The labourers in the village demanded more wages. This was a problem for the landlords as well. 'We can somehow manage now, but how do we cope with work during the harvest?' This was the main concern. Some others thought, 'What can really grow in that land filled with rocks? Someone has misguided them. They will come for the harvest on their own.' The drunkards in Kalluru were upset because they were deprived of liquor.

Thukya, who was working for Gowda, informed him of all the happenings in the Thanda. 'That teacher who has come to the Thanda has been going from house to house requesting people to send their children to school. Besides, he has a role in influencing the people to cultivate the grazing grounds. Nothing good will come out of it, sir. Our people will eat humble pie for listening to his advice.' Gowda had begun to discuss the matter with the people of the village.

I also got to know of all the news in circulation. I approached Somalya and told him all I knew. 'Master, don't get frightened. What have you done? Have you done anything unwarranted? You have just encouraged us a little. Don't worry, we are with you,' he assured me.

Fourteen

I went home for summer vacations. Everyone in my village eagerly asked, 'How do you manage to live in that Thanda?' They did not believe me when I told them that I was happy. My mother, having found a suitable match for my younger sister, started pestering me to get married in her eagerness to bring home a daughter-in-law. When I said that I had just got a job and will need a couple of years to settle down, my sister taunted mischievously, 'Perhaps he has found someone in the Thanda.'

'Are you up to something like that?' asked mother, half mockingly, half seriously. I recalled how I was attracted to Ruplibai's daughter. But that girl had showed no interest in me. She would talk to me affectionately merely because I was her teacher. For a moment, I began to wonder how she was, away from her parents and living a life of her own.

When I returned to the Thanda after the vacations, monsoon had already set in. It rained continuously in the Thanda. There had never been such heavy rains in the past. It was rain worth witnessing. The lake filled to the brim. Since the huts in the Thanda were leaking, many people took shelter in the school. They were never deterred by the odds they had to face. They felt happy as the lake was filled with water to the brim and the lands could be irrigated to grow crops.

One evening, Damla came to the school. 'Master, we have begun our work. Seeds have to be sown in the fields on an auspicious day. Only Kasanu, Somalya and Khubya have bullocks. The fields to be ploughed are very large. I too want to buy a pair of bullocks. Can you get me a loan from somewhere? It has rained well with the blessings of Mariyamma. The lake is full. If we reap a rich harvest with what we sow, who can subdue us?'

I did not know how to respond to his questions. How can I get him a loan? Though I knew it was impossible, I felt a little uneasy looking at the man who had come to me with much enthusiasm and lots of hope and definite plans for the future. 'It is a good idea that you want to sow seeds in your part of the land, which has been well prepared. But how is it possible to buy a pair of bullocks immediately? It is possible to delay a little the sowing of seeds. Anyway, the lands will be irrigated by the water stored in the lake. You retain the seeds for sowing and sell the rest. This will give you some money. When the lands are divided and you get your share, then you should plan to buy bullocks,' I advised him. I'm not sure if he liked what I said. He got up and left the place, murmuring to himself.

I went to the temple. Limbya was coming from the opposite side with a sullen look on his face. 'I was coming to you,' he said.

'What's the matter?' I asked.

'Nothing in particular, just like that,' he responded.

I began to wonder what was troubling him. And as we walked along, he began to open up, 'The other day, the elders of the panchayat had a meeting and came to a decision. The marriage is to be celebrated soon.'

'Inform Nayak about this,' I suggested.

'I'm afraid of talking to him. He is an elderly person and he may say anything he likes. If he says something when not in good mood, he will stand by it forever – I want you to talk to him,' he said.

'Ok. I shall talk to him when I meet him at the platform,' I assured him.

Somalya came to the platform after offering his prayers at

the temple. His face was beaming with a sense of satisfaction after having accomplished a major task. I approached him with my usual complaint, 'It has been a week since the school has reopened; children are yet to come to school.'

'Your school cannot run according to its schedule here. It is the sowing season. You have to make adjustments according to the circumstances of the Thanda. What else can I say to you? Ok, the sowing work will be over in four-five days. After that we will look into the matter of sending the children to school,' he said.

He added, 'If every one of us had bullocks, the sowing work could have been completed by now.' I told him that Damla had approached me for a loan to buy bullocks. 'Don't mind my saying this, master. He always behaves like that. But he has now given up stealing and drinking and has mended his ways. He is now attracted to land and agriculture. He has prepared his portion of the land well. Besides this, our people have given up the liquor trade and begun to depend on the land. I feel those days are not far when our life of poverty and difficulties will be at an end. We are planning to perform Limbya's marriage immediately after the sowing season. Duglibai, Rukki, Limbya and his mother are all working very well together in the fields. I don't need to make any special mention of the involvement of the youth,' he said. This saved me from having to broach the topic of Limbya's marriage.

Fifteen

A month must have passed since the sowing work was over. The grazing grounds were no longer fallow but looked cheerful, with a green cover. The large piece of land that was dry and abandoned was endowed with life now. People's faces were bright with smiles like freshly tinseled vessels.

By now, the people of the Thanda had started to prepare for the marriage of Rukki and Limbya. This was not a marriage involving just two families. This was a festive occasion where the entire Thanda would participate as one family. This was a marriage of a rare kind. Though Somalya by nature was conservative, he had a fairly liberal attitude towards this union. He had shown generosity in matters related to the marriage of Rukki and Limbya. Rather than generosity, it would be proper to say that it was an expression of affection and love he had for this girl. 'We don't need to observe all the formalities of a conventional marriage. It is enough if we declare them man and wife,' opined some of the elders. Some others were vehement, 'How can it be considered a marriage unless some of the basic rituals are observed?' As the chief of the Thanda, Somalya took a leading role in the discussions. He also had to assume the role of bride's father while Ruplibai had to take on the role of her mother. Duglibai could not take up the responsibilities of the marriage directly. Loku had to be convinced to take up the role of Rukki's brother. Since both the bride and the groom belonged

to the Thanda, there was no need for anyone to go out of the settlement. Kasanu happily agreed to be the companion of the groom and go to the bride's house with him.

Though senior in age, Kasanu had a good sense of humour. He could mingle with the youngsters and become young himself and have fun. He would ask them riddles and challenge them to solve them. 'Angadi macheni, takadim tholeni, orasayi pooja veni? (What is it that is not sold in a shop, nor weighed on scales, but without which there can be no worshipping of gods?)' No youngster was able to answer this riddle and pestered him, 'Tell us what it is. Tell us what it is.' Finally, when they accepted their defeat, he revealed, 'Cow dung'. He was a simple and unassuming person. During Holi Purnima (full moon), he would sing the lenghi songs all through the night.

Kasanu, who was nearly six-feet tall, would find the width of dhoti a little too short for him. I have been a witness to Kasanu, with oval face and long nose, wearing a blue turban and singing melodiously with his eyes closed and a hand on his ear. This man now had to act as the groom's companion. The companion is called leriya and he is to act somewhat like a jester, a friend of the groom. When the in-laws and other relatives make verbal attacks on the groom or taunt him, the leriya is supposed to defend him and negotiate the situation tactfully. Kasanu was, in many ways, best suited for this job.

Limbya's parents and relatives, Somalya and his wife and the elders of the Thanda went to Duglibai's house for marriage negotiations. The dark-complexioned Limbya tried his best to keep his straight upright hair well groomed. He had buttoned his shirt and rolled down his sleeves, which were otherwise always rolled up. After the groom's party was seated in Duglibai's house, the two parties exchanged kothalis (embroidered bags). The bag given to the bride's party was filled with fenugreek, fennel seeds and copra while the bag given to the groom's party was filled with jaggery and jowar. Once this ceremony was over, everyone gathered in front of Somalya's house. On the suggestion of one of the elders, the parents of the bride and groom wished for each other's welfare.

panch panchat raj bhojer sabha
sagal kacheri pachare laakh
ana pacheri savya laakh
ke sag sag kaader mod

'We, the parents of the bride and the groom, mutually agree to have this wedding solemnized. Though the plants and trees abound in thorns, they bear fruits mixed with sweetness and flavour; our relationship shall be similar. Let our families mingle like honey and milk. May our relationship be like the fruit hidden behind the leaves in a tree. Can the two ears of a horse be similar? Let us know that a ladder made of leather lasts longer than a ladder made of wood. Greens sprout from the earth with raindrops that fall from the sky. Let us consume those greens and bond together. May this bond sustain for seven generations to come.'

Limbya was baptized at his house before the marriage ceremony. According to custom, a groom is considered fit for marriage only after he is baptized by being branded with a piece of hot iron. Married women sang religious songs as Somalya pierced one end of a jowar stalk with a needle, heated it till red hot and branded Limbya on his right shoulder. He recited the Gayathri Mantram seven times and chanted the spell of Guru Sai, 'koli aav, koli java, koli maayi, sada sada. (Seven cocks here, and another seven there – referring to the exchange of cocks between the groom's mother and the village head.)'

Let no shadows darken the bright lamp of our relationship, Oh groom, may you be protected by Guru Gosai.

Once the ceremony was complete, he advised the groom, 'You should work like a bullet issued from a rifle.'

The groom was dressed like a leader, a chief, in a red shirt, a red turban, a red shawl wrapped around his shoulders, a belt on his waist, a copper or a silver ring on each finger, earrings, a silver bracelet on his forearm, a bag with betel leaves tied to a side, a silver waist band and a woolen skein. All the embellishments had given Limbya a special glow. When he was brought to the pandal erected in the veranda, his mother and sisters embraced him and started crying as if he was deserting them forever.

Limbya got ready to proceed to the bride's place after Somalya Nayak had offered him fruit juice and khichdi. It was obligatory on his part to visit the bride's house, get married to her and return to his house with her in tow. Kasanu was also ready to go with him as his companion. If the bride had belonged to another thanda, the companion would have had to go there too with the groom. As per tradition, the companion led Limbya to the bride's house. Limbya went ahead, looking like a brave soldier with a sword in his hand, giving the impression that he was prepared to remove any obstacle in the way before entering the battlefield that was wedlock.

The groom and his retinue first went to the temple of Sevalal. The bride's people had not yet arrived to welcome the party. The companion, after visiting Somalya's house and exchanging greetings, sent for the people from Rukki's house. Ruplibai, in the company of a few girls, went out to welcome the guests. Ruplibai untied the bundle of goodies the groom had brought with him and distributed them among everyone. The two parties got together and started singing traditional wedding songs, some funny, some bawdy. Both the groom and the companion were offered water. The companion accepted the water, murmuring his thanks. The bride's party teased him, insisting that he repeat his appreciation clearly and expressly. There was an atmosphere of fun and hilarity, with guests from either party teasing each other, clapping and laughing loudly. It was as if the whole Thanda was laughing and dancing with joy.

Everyone gathered in front of Rukki's house. The groom and

the companion were made to sit on a mat and asked a few teasing questions, 'Who are you? Why have you come? How did you come?' The companion responded to these questions in the form of a riddle. But the group was not satisfied with his answer and as a punishment for this he was made to distribute betel leaves and nuts to everyone. As he was engaged in this task, children were made to sit on his bent back. When he said, 'Please have the betel leaves, please have the nuts,' everyone burst into laughter.

At an opportune moment, when the companion had stepped away, Rukki's friends came and ushered Limbya respectfully into the house and asked him to occupy an elevated place and not sit on the ground. They said, 'We have stacked these bags and spread a carpet to help you sit in comfort.' Just as he was about to sit down, the companion rushed in and sensing mischief, pulled the carpet and exposed the secret. The bag was filled with dry chillies. Everyone burst into laughter. The girls felt cheated. The companion had saved Limbya from an embarrassment, but this did not stop the girls from singing a song to tease him.

vethadu hate math bes
marchar pothapar bes
tharo dilmil baliyatho
manmath bes

(Groom, don't sit on the ground
Perch high on the bag of chillies
If your behind burns, say it to none.)

The elders decided to have the thilak ceremony the same night instead of postponing it to the next day. When Loku, assuming the role of her brother, applied thilak on Rukki's forehead, some sad songs were sung. Rukki felt comforted at the thought of having been saved from Lachamya by Nayak and the people of the Thanda. But she was sad that she had to move away from her mother's house. The free bird that she was here had fears about her life in her husband's house and became emotional. Limbya was not a stranger. But she was not sure how he would treat her after becoming her husband. How would his aged father and mother treat her! She must have been troubled by such anxieties. Perhaps this was why she had tears in her eyes when she sang the song.

> *math lagadore ee renaa*
> *ini chuni haldeero teeko*
> *thamaj lagaadiya tho*
> . . . .
> . . . .

> (Brother, don't put that yellow thilak you have brought
> If you put this, your sister will be somebody else's.
> Alas! Even when I plead, you put the thilak on my forehead.
> Putting this dot why do you keep me away?
> Leaving the path strewn with flowers
> Have I to tread these stony and thorny paths?)

The marriage was to be solemnized the next day. The special feature here was that all ceremonies were held on full moon nights. Two pestles were dug in the ground at some distance from each other in the front yard. A pair of nutmegs, cowries and tender roots of turmeric were all tied with a black thread to the end of each pestle. In the four corners of the pandal, seven earthen pots were stacked on top of one another. Each pot was whitewashed with lime and motifs were drawn on them. All around them were festoons of green leaves and branches of yucca plant. Perhaps this indicated a wish that life should be prosperous and evergreen.

A round, wooden, upturned dish was placed close to the pestle and the bride was made to sit on that and given a bath. It was a wonderful sight. When it was the groom's turn to sit on the same upturned dish, Ruplibai, who had assumed the role of bride's mother, came and anointed his hair with oil and poured water over his head. She poured water on his head while combing his hair; she collected the water flowing down his body in her cupped hands and drank it. Both the parties were singing songs and making fun of each other. When he was being given a bath, a few girls tried to pull the dish from under him and upset his balance. However, Kasanu the companion whispered something in his ear and made sure he would not budge. The companion was helpful in preventing the groom from being harassed by the bride's party and guarding the prestige of the groom's party.

Even while he was wearing the dhoti, he was made to stand on the inverted wooden dish as a test of his strength and skill. Ruplibai, as his mother-in-law, held pebbles in both her hands and asked him to 'make a promise' and say as follows, 'I will look after your daughter well; I will never scold or use harsh words with my mother-in-law and my wife.' As he made this promise, he with his tender moustache, laughed on the other side of the mouth.

Limbya sat tightly crouched after he had his bath. 'Why is he sitting like this, in a lump? Can't he sit properly?' I asked a person who was standing near me. 'He has to face one more test to prove his prowess,' the man responded, laughing. The test began. Two girls fetched the skirt discarded by Rukki after her bath and began to try and shove it under his armpits. When he refused to relax his arms, a girl tickled him causing him to immediately loosen up, and the girls succeeded in their efforts. Shouts of 'loser, loser' emanating from the bride's party filled the air. 'You shouldn't tickle. Cheating, cheating,' protested the groom's party. Somalya appeased both parties and made way for furthering the ceremonies. Though Somalya had assumed the role of the bride's father, playing a leading role in performing the marriage rituals, there seemed to be some sadness writ large on his face. Perhaps he was sorry that his own daughter's marriage could not be celebrated in this manner.

The elders decided to have the mangalya dharana (the ceremony where the groom ties a trinket around the wife's neck) the same night rather than the next morning. Rukki gave up her old clothes and put on the clothes given to her by the groom. She also wore bangles and jewels to go with the mangalyam. When Ruplibai embraced her and cried, she sang the sad songs of parting. After all the ceremonies were over and food was served to appease the departed souls of forefathers, everyone present was served. A ram was sacrificed and after everyone had their fill of food and drink, the ceremonies came to an end.

As Rukki was leaving with Limbya, she fell on the feet of Somalya and cried bitterly. 'I have never seen my father, but you have been more than a father to me,' she wept. In response, Somalya said, 'I have not done anything more than I should. Don't cry. Take heart. Limbya is a good person. His mother and father are old people. Look after your husband and your parents-in-law well.' He then blessed her, saying, 'Be happy.' He also blessed Limbya when he touched his feet. 'Both of you be happy,' he said. Rukki embraced Rupli and began to cry. She sang the haveli (traditional parting song) with a heavy heart.

haveliye aahinya
maaroj bapuri haveli aahinya
harirese hariyaali rese

Let my Thanda prosper and grow
Like the shoots of grass growing along the river bank
May you live in harmony like the honey dissolving in milk
Let your tribe prosper and grow like a banyan or a peepal;
I take leave of you and go away from here
But let my Thanda prosper with every season
And provide comfort and happiness to everyone.

The women were crying, holding on to each other. Perhaps Ruplibai was overwhelmed with memories of her own daughter.

Others perhaps remembered their daughters who had been married off to grooms in other thandas. I was very surprised on witnessing the traditions and cultural richness of these people in celebrating a marriage. I wondered how deep-seated the roots of tradition were among these nomads.

While everyone was busy with the festivities some shouts were heard at a distance. 'There seems to be some noise. Who's shouting?' the people gathered enquired anxiously. Some of them began to run towards the fields. Someone shouted, 'Cattle from Kalluru have entered our fields!' Limbya looked disturbed and uneasy as he stood there. A little while later, the youngsters of the Thanda came running, swearing by their prowess. They explained that some of the Kalluru youngsters had let loose their cattle in the fields and were sitting calmly outside as the Thanda boys rushed to drive the cattle away. The Thanda youngsters got into a fight with these boys and the two groups of youngsters beat each other up.

'It was good that we beat them; that should send a warning. We should retort; otherwise they will trample on us, these village people!' said one of the elders. In response, the boys said with pride, 'We have made sure that they will never come this side again.' Somalya tried to guess the intention behind the move. 'If so many heads of cattle were let loose at one time, there must have been some cunning scheme behind it. Some elders also expressed similar doubts...Let us face what comes our way. Let us not lose courage,' he said. When I suggested, 'Why don't you lodge a police complaint?' Somalya interrupted and said, 'Wait, let us not be the first to go to the police.'

The people of the Thanda, who had so far been immersed in the wedding ceremonies, contracted like touch-me-not plants after this bitter incident.

Sixteen

'It was dark, pitch dark. It was so dark that I could not even see my own forearm. In the midst of such darkness, there was suddenly a dazzling flash of light. The darkness disappeared at once and the world was visible again. Sevalal, the celibate, the very incarnation of truth, arrived riding on a white horse, wearing a golden crown. I prostrated myself before him with my hands folded and addressed him as the great one who resides in the hearts of people he loves. I prayed for prosperity. The white horse moved slowly, and stopped near me and shook its body. The great person lifted his hand to bless me and said, "My lad, my blessings are with you." Once this was uttered, the white horse began to trot away. How can I express my happiness! – I was woken up suddenly. I sat up and offered my obeisance to the great one silently and lay down to go back to sleep...Once again, it was very dark, but the scenario was very different. There were clouds thundering in the sky. It appeared that a war was ensuing in the heavens. Bright red embers began to rain down on the earth. It was as if a giant measuring the earth and heavens stood there. Then, Mariyamma appeared, riding a roaring lion. I prayed to her to save me. The Goddess questioned, "Have you forgotten me?" "No, mother, how can I forget you?" I said.

'I woke up drenched in sweat, even though a cool breeze was blowing. I removed my sweat-soaked shirt and stood bare-chested in the cool breeze. Tiny stars were twinkling in the sky.

At the break of dawn, I ran to the priest's place and narrated my dreams to him. I asked him to interpret it. "Arrange for the procession of the goddess, everything will be all right," he said.

'I had a sense of satisfaction. The reason is: Somalya was blessed with the vision of Sevalal. I was also equally frightened. That is because, there was a giant standing in that frightening darkness. We have to break his head and tame him. To achieve this, I need the blessings and help from Mariyamma. We have to seek her blessings. What do you say, master? What is your opinion?'

When Somalya shared his dreams and feelings with me, master did not have any response. I did not want to hurt his feelings.

❖

Hari completed his B.Com and reported for work as a clerk in the District Cooperative Bank before returning to the Thanda. Everyone was both happy and surprised. He had met Bhim Singh, a Lambada and the Director of Vijayapura Bank, through Hiralal and it was on his recommendation that he had got the job. He was the first person among the people from the Thanda to be highly qualified and get a job. His father, Somalya, was very happy and his heart swelled with pride. The whole Thanda felt proud of him. Somalya wanted people to get educated and become free from poverty. But he felt that along with such progress, they should continue to uphold their traditions and culture.

He was in some ways committed to traditions, but in certain aspects he was quite progressive. It is difficult to assess how he acquired this progressive bent of mind. Though he was progressive, he was upset when I had got a blouse stitched for his daughter. He seemed to realize that education was essential to achieve economic development and to get rid of the liquor trade and the complementary trade of prostitution. When it came to such issues, he would behave in a progressive manner and take the elders into confidence.

Loku felt happy at the achievement of his brother Hari. But he had regrets as he had come back without completing his education. 'What if I am not educated, I shall be more prosperous than him,' he boasted in my presence.

Kasanu's wife, Lalibai, made lapsi (sweet dish) and invited Hari for lunch. There was a deep friendship between the two families. Somalya had more respect and concern for Kasanu's father, Ramji, than he had for his own father. In fact, he did not have any respect for his father. This is because he was always engaged in singing, dancing, drinking and other forms of entertainment. He never thought of saving some money to make life comfortable. Somalya's mother was largely responsible for his acquiring good habits. Unlike his father, Ramji had been a positive influence on him. The bond of friendship between the two families had continued to this day. When Hari had finished his lunch, Ramji told him, 'Your father has struggled a lot. He has selflessly worked for the progress of the entire Thanda. You have earned a job, but don't forget your mother, father and this Thanda.'

Hari left for Vijayapura after staying in the Thanda for three or four days. Kasanu teased Somalya, 'So now you will get ready to go to town with your son.'

'What will I do in that town without all of you? My work is here. I have to work and strive in this soil,' Somalya responded.

Ruplibai seemed to be saddened that her son did not stay on for a longer period. As he was leaving, she embraced him and began to cry loudly. 'Why, what has happened to you? Where is he going? For a job! If you want, you can go with him,' Somalya said in a loud voice. Then, in a gentler voice, he said, 'Bless your son and wish him health and happiness wherever he may be.' This consoled her.

❖

A few days passed by. Nothing special happened. One day, a young man named Jagadish, clad in a khadi Nehru shirt and pajamas arrived at the Thanda, riding a noisy motorbike. People of all ages immediately gathered around him. He expressed his concern about the Thanda to the elders and said, 'Panchayat elections are due and our party has decided to field the youth. The youth here need to be ready,' he said.

'We don't understand this election-pelection. If you are looking for young men from the Thanda, take them aside and talk to them,' said Somalya and sent them all away. All of them went to the platform of Mariyamma's temple.

'Select one among you and give me the name. There is a seat for the Thanda. I shall suggest this name on behalf of my party. It is not right for you to remain cocooned in your own world today. You have to be in touch with the outside world. The days of those elders are over. They have already placed one foot in the grave and the other is still outside. You should prepare yourselves now. Only then will your Thanda progress. There is another important matter. In a week's time, the honourable minister will visit Nagarkote. We shall send a lorry to the Thanda then. If all of you, boys and girls, come there, you will also be noticed. You should all come without fail,' he said.

The young people gathered there said, 'Please tell this to our elders, then we can all come.' They also suggested, 'Loku is our leader, write down his name.' All of them returned to the platform under the neem tree. Jagadish approached the elders and said, 'Elders, since the honourable minister is visiting Nagarkote, it gives you an opportunity to put forth your requests. For that, all of you from the Thanda should come. You should show your strength. We shall arrange for a lorry to fetch you and return you to the Thanda. There will also be arrangements made for lunch and snacks. Without any worry, you can get into the lorry as soon as it arrives and come over. Since the honourable minister's speech begins exactly at ten, it is better for all of you to come as early as possible.'

Jagadish's proposal was discussed by all the elders and they concluded that this was a good opportunity to discuss the problem of the grazing grounds with a minister. The elders assured him that every one of them would come.

As promised, a lorry drove up to the Thanda on the designated morning. I also got ready to go when Somalya requested me to accompany them, saying, 'It will be better if you also join us, master. You come and put us in touch with Hiralal; that will suffice.' Somalya went to Sevalal's temple and Mariyamma's temple to seek blessings before getting into the lorry. The driver was urging everyone to get in quickly, saying, 'Leaving the aged and toddlers, the rest of you get in quickly. Stand close to each other. Women sit down. Okay, sister, sit down. Okay, lady, get back a little.' With such commands, the driver packed everyone into the lorry like sheep.

Along the way, they looked at the verdant green crops, noting that the crops they had grown were better, and felt proud. With the blessings of Sevalal and the kindness of Mariyamma if the land they have tilled becomes their own, there could be no end to their prosperity, this was everyone's dream.

We reached Nagarkote. The lorry offloaded us on the border of the town and disappeared. We had to cut across the town and walk a distance of three kilometers to the field where the minister was to make his speech. As we passed by the hotels and the tall multi-storey buildings, men and women stopped and stared at them with awe and wonder. 'How much money they must have amassed, master!' remarked Damla.

'When our thatched roof leaks during monsoon, we do not have the resources to re-thatch it. How much money could have been spent in building these?' joined in two others. When they saw a big cutout of an actor in front of a cinema theatre, the women were surprised and got rooted to the spot, saying 'Hai, Hai' with their hands on their mouth. They were in a state of wonder as if they were transported to a different world. Loku was instructing all of them to keep to a side of the road without obstructing the movement of cars, buses, lorries and autos. When Loku reprimanded them, saying, 'Will you walk quickly, or do you want to stay put here on the road?' the women slowly moved forward.

The people of the town were gazing down at the hordes of people who had arrived from the Thanda from the windows and doors of their multistoried homes. When they realized that they were being watched, the women and girls felt shy and adjusted their veils. When some uncouth men remarked, 'Look at the beautiful "goods" passing by,' Damla got enraged and dragged two of the men out and slapped them hard. Being worried about a fight ensuing, I said, 'Leave it alone, we don't have to care for what everyone says.'

'We should not let these people go unpunished, master. We should thrash them; it is only then they will learn to behave,' he said.

Loku and his friends were walking in the front of the group, with long strides. Somalya, a few others and I were in the middle. The women were scattered here and there. Rukki stopped in front of a huge clothing store where two beautiful mannequins draped in saris and blouses were placed attractively at the store display window. Mesmerised by the mannequins, which closely resembled living women, and by the saris and blouses they wore, she stood there, transfixed. A young man riding a motorbike came from nowhere and stopped near her and began to pester her, saying, 'I am Rangaraju, the son-in-law of the excise contractor. Don't you recognize me? When I came for a ride, I saw you. If you want that saree, take it; I will buy it for you. Live with me, I will keep you in comfort. Why do you want to live in that hovel of the Thanda? I will put you up in a house of your own and treat you like a queen.' He used all and the tricks known to him and tried to woo her. 'Get on the vehicle,' he insisted.

Rukki was aghast. She screamed out loud, 'Oh Limbya!' People in the crowded market turned to look at her and some of them enquired what had happened. At this, Rangaraju high-tailed it on his motorcycle at full speed. She ran and joined the group, gasping for breath. Limbya enquired, 'What happened?' With tears flowing from her eyes she said, 'That bastard, scum of the earth, scoundrel! What does he think of me?' After using expletives for a while, she narrated the entire incident to Limbya as it had happened. 'Didn't I tell you? This is a town. Terribly crowded! Didn't I ask all of you to stick together? If we had come across him in the Thanda we could have thrashed him; there are several roads through which he can escape here,' he said, expressing his inability to punish the man. 'Stick together,' Limbya warned Rukki and also looked at other young boys and girls sharply. He made sure they understood him. 'These people will not allow us to be ourselves and be happy,' Ruplibai reacted. Some were aware of this incident and some were not.

We reached the open-air space where the assembly was being organized. A large number of people clad in khadi shirts, dhotis and caps had assembled. Cars were arriving in large numbers. Jagadish, who had come to invite us at the Thanda, was nowhere to be seen. Neither could we find Hiralal. I looked for the organizers. They had made arrangements for snacks and tea for the people who had been brought from outside. I made everyone stand in a queue and got them tea and a packet of chooda (beaten rice). As we had left the Thanda early in the morning, everyone was hungry. After eating chooda in quick mouthfuls and sipping tea, some spirit was restored in everyone.

Though the minister's speech was scheduled for ten in the morning, he did not arrive till noon. I left these people in one place and went in search of Hiralal. Nobody was able to give me correct information about him. When I teased Loku by asking him, 'Where is the youth leader, Jagadish, who asked all of you to come here?' he looked a little pale.

From the dais there was an announcement, 'The Honourable Minister is due to arrive in a few minutes. He has been delayed as he was felicitated in a nearby village. All of you are requested to cooperate.' I would feel more confident if I could meet Hiralal. I was feeling depressed, not knowing what to do with these people. Several hours passed with the announcements at regular intervals assuring the arrival of the minister 'in a few minutes'. Hiralal made his appearance all of a sudden. I could breathe easy now. He said, 'I went to talk to the PA and seek an appointment with the minister. I have been informed that we may meet him in the Inspection Bungalow at 8 p.m. What have you been doing till now?'

'What can we do? We are sitting here, just waiting,' Somalya replied. Somalya the leader and other elders who were very important people in the Thanda were now aghast. The cars, the large dais, the announcements on the loudspeakers – all of it made them feel lost. As soon as Hiralal arrived, Loku, Dhenya and the other youngsters assumed the role of volunteers and began to move around here and there. The ruling party had arranged this programme. It seemed that they had organized the meet to give an account of their achievements and also appeal to the people to return them to power once again in the next elections.

The party workers began to distribute the handbills and party flags made of paper. The convener of the programme began to give instructions to the gathered public, 'The honourable minister is about to arrive; as soon as he arrives I will shout out the name of the party and all of you should respond with "Jai!" Similarly, each time I mention the name of the minister, you should applaud loudly.'

The minister's car eventually arrived, with a beacon on top, making a screeching noise. Several cars and police vans arrived before and after the minister's car, all making a lot of noise. There was a murmur and stir among the people, 'The minister has arrived, the minister has arrived!' As the minister was getting on the dais, several white caps began to move around him. As soon as the convener came to the microphone the people began to applaud. Once the noise subsided and the programme was about to begin, Hiralal shouted, 'Banjara Association!' This was met with a resounding 'Jai!' from Loku and his friends. Perhaps Hiralal had tutored them in advance. Everyone's attention was drawn to them. From the dais information about who they were was sought and 'leave them alone, leave them alone,' was the generous remark passed. As soon as the police came and threatened to arrest them, they broke into a cold sweat.

Before the minister began his speech, various leaders came and praised him for his efficiency. Finally, the minister began his speech. 'Beloved friends of my constituency, the achievements of our government in the last four years are well known to you all. I have to admit with regret that the people in the opposition have only been critical of the good work we have been doing without offering any help constructively in nation building. We have ushered in several programmes to alleviate poverty. We have been following the path of Mahatma Gandhi, the father of the nation. How can we forget the people who have sacrificed their lives for independence? I want to say proudly that we are striving to make their dreams a reality while remembering their sacrifices with gratitude. The progress of the poor is our motto; we need to lift the last man, the most oppressed one. We propose to redistribute the lands. In this regard, our coordinator is going to call a meeting of all the thinking heads in the capital city.' He went on rambling. There was applause for everything he said.

Somalya was excited. He dreamt of a prosperous future and imagined that heaven was within his reach. He thought if he could meet the minister in person through the good offices of Hiralal and petition his request, it would definitely be fulfilled.

As soon as the minister finished his speech, people began to follow him. The cars began to move with a whirr. Since the appointment with the minister was at eight, it was decided that a few could stay back for the meeting and the rest could be sent back to the Thanda. They had waited the whole day for the speech in the sun having only had some chooda for breakfast. We had to arrange for the evening snacks. We requested the volunteers to arrange a lorry for Havan. Nobody was inclined to listen to us after the programme was over. Like us, other groups of people who had been brought over from the neighbouring areas were also worried. There was no option but for everyone to stay back. Hiralal, Somalya and I managed to get some churmuri (puffed rice) and chooda. For the hungry stomachs, this was grossly inadequate. Ravanana hottige kaasina majjige – It is impossible to satiate hungry stomachs. People began to settle down for the night in the field. This was not unusual for the people of the Thanda. But that day these nomads had come without any preparation, submitting themselves to the mercy of others.

After everyone was supplied with chooda and water, Hiralal said, 'All of you lie down here under the banyan tree. Four to six of us will go to the Inspection Bunglow IB.' Damla sat in the midst of the girls and boys, making jokes and teasing them. Somalya, Kasanu, Hiralal, Loku, Dhenya and I went to the IB. Several people were already there, waiting to meet the minister. We did not get an appointment though it was past eight. 'The minister is now meeting the officials; you have to wait a little longer,' said his personal staff. 'Come, let us go and sit there,' said Hiralal, leading us to a corner.

'This minister was drowned in loans and litigations before he was elected. Look at him now. In these four years he has become quite well-off. He has earned enough for the next seven generations of his family to live in comfort. He has built bungalows and big buildings in Bangalore. He exploits the weaknesses of the officials and plays with them. He collects his regular 'cuts' from them every month. It is not just him, but his followers also need to receive the share of cuts. The roads get repaired on paper all through the year. All the funds are swallowed by them. Who is there to question all this? Who has the courage to ask? Even if someone asks, what changes are likely to happen? What huge sums each one extracts! They talk of uplifting the poor, what upliftment do they bring about? All bullshit! How can the project coordinators get to know the difficulties of the poor? They visit America and try to implement foreign strategies of development here, fools. They hold their meetings in five-star hotels in air-conditioned rooms. Everything is nonsense. Only he who is wise nowadays can have his fill.'

Somalya was taken aback by these stinging remarks from Hiralal. Frightened by his words and feeling a little disappointed, he asked, 'Will the minister be helpful to us or not?'

'All this depends on how forcefully we put in our appeal. Did you notice how, when we shouted in the meeting, the minister asked for us to be left alone when he heard my name? How do you think this happened? I am a well-known leader among the labourers. They know my strength. We shouted to register our strength. It does not pay to be simple-minded these days.'

These matters were beyond the comprehension of Somalya and Kasanu. But Loku seemed to understand this.

After the minister concluded his meeting with the officials, Hiralal was called in. I stayed outside. The rest went in with him. Hiralal made a petition and explained to the minister how the Lambadas have been settled in the Thanda for a long time. They need to be given possession of the grazing grounds adjacent to their settlement so that they can begin to cultivate the same. The minister immediately asked his PA to send a note to the revenue section. When Hiralal reminded him that the application submitted to the District Collector had received no response, the minister instructed his people to take necessary action. The people of the Thanda paid their respects to the minister and came out, feeling happy. Hiralal explained to me everything that had happened and said he had to go to the factory in the morning. He instructed us, 'Take a lorry going towards Kalluru early in the morning,' and left. We all returned to the platform under the banyan tree. Kasanu, Somalya and myself said to ourselves that we need to leave the place early in the morning and walked towards the dais to sleep. The rest lay down wherever they were.

Early next morning, we reached the road and hailed lorries that could take us to the Kalluru crossroads, in batches. From there, we had to get to the Thanda on foot. By the time we reached, we were all exhausted.

Seventeen

Word of our meeting with the minister began to spread in Kalluru. The villagers heard that people from the Thanda had given him a petition to cultivate the grazing grounds and received assurances in return.

It is believed that originally the grazing grounds belonged to the Desais. However, they had given up these lands two generations ago either because they were beyond the visible distance from the village, or out of sheer generosity, so that the cattle could graze there. When the senior Desai had been alive, Manya Nayak had brought his people along to him, seeking work. They were employed to work in the fields of Desai, Gowda and Kulkarni. Somalya, when he was a young boy, would take the cattle out to graze. When he grew up, he began to work in their fields, harnessing the bullocks. Somalya and the members of his family were trusted by the Desais.

When Manya Nayak arrived with his troupe of people, the natives of Kalluru wondered why Desai had invited such people. Those were the times when people firmly believed that the Lambadas were deft at stealing sheep from the sheds and were drunkards, liars and scoundrels. But as days passed, these people won the confidence of Desai and others with their hard work and honesty. The people of Kalluru realized that the Lambadas would give up their lives for those who trusted them. Some of them began to work on a regular basis in the fields and gardens of landlords. But it was only during the harvest season that everyone in the Thanda would work in Kalluru. During this season, the Lambadas were more important than the village guards, shepherds and scavengers. This is because the labourers in the village would complete the work in their own small plots of land first and then come to work for others. But the Lambadas would stay put in the fields and would not leave till all the work was completed. They would ensure the crops and hay would reach the stacks before the onset of the rains. They would take up all kinds of work, such as reaping jowar, heaping the ears with corn, piling them up in stacks and work day and night till everything was done. In this manner, an inseparable bond developed between the people of the Thanda and Kalluru.

But of late, this bond seemed to have developed cracks. The elders of Kalluru and the neighbouring villages often complained about the young men who would visit the Thanda to drink liquor. They felt that the Thanda was spoiling their young by giving them access to liquor. Some of the women in the village also suspected the elders of smuggling liquor into the village for their own consumption and having illicit relationships with the women of the Thanda who brewed liquor. But these issues were not so important.

Once the senior Desai passed away, his two children upon completing their education went to the city. One went to Mumbai while the other reached Hubballi. As the crops grown here did not reach either of them, they decided to sell their land. It is believed that at that time Somalya asked them, 'Give me four or five acres of land. I shall pay you the money later.' In response they said, 'We shall not divide the land into small pieces and sell it. We want to sell the entire land in one piece. So, it's not possible.' Somalya suppressed his desire and kept quiet. After a few days, Desai's children also sold their palace-like house and went away to the city without ever looking back at the village.

The strong desire to own a piece of land and cultivate it as farmers never diminished in Somalya and his companions. They would look for any ray of hope that was visible. Somalya nursed dreams of his people living independently by cultivating the grazing grounds and putting an end to the liquor trade and the prostitution that was so closely associated with it. He thought it would be a boon to the entire community. This had been his dream.

The dream had now become a reality, and the grazing grounds were being cultivated by the Lambadas. They were getting ready for the harvest. The people of Kalluru were convinced that these Lambadas would not help them with their harvest. When they realized that the people of the Thanda, who used to come in hordes as farm labourers, would no longer be available this year, they began to worry. When a couple of Lambadas were asked if they would be helping out at the village, they said unhesitatingly, 'How is that possible? Let us first finish harvesting our fields and then we'll see.'

The small farmers did not bother much about this. They could somehow manage by themselves. But the landlords of big holdings were taken aback. Venkanna Gowda, Bandurao Kulkarni, Basettappa, Hanuma Reddy and other landlords gathered to discuss the matter. With Panchayati Raj coming into effect, though Gowda and Kulkarni had lost much of their power, they had not given up their pride. People with wealth and large pieces of land are always important in a society. All such people, with their supporters, met in one place on a certain day. I do not know for certain who said what, but by and large this was the discussion:

'It is our fault to have allowed them to cultivate up to this stage.'

'When I had mentioned that they had begun to cultivate the grazing grounds, Gowda had said rather uninterestedly, what can they grow in that fallow land?'

'On average, they are said to get a minimum of ten sacks of

jowar per acre. If we calculate the entire produce in the grazing grounds, we should not be surprised if it is more than what Gowda and Kulkarni will have.'

'In that case, they will buy this Gowda and Kulkarni.'

'Let bygones be bygones, what should we do now?'

'The grazing grounds are not registered as agriculture lands. This is an illegal activity.'

'We should lodge a police complaint against this, we should write an application, and we should also go and meet the minister.'

'The minister seems to have assured them of granting those lands to them.'

'Is the minister an outsider to us? Has he planned to get all the votes of the Lambadas en bloc?'

'If all the people in the village get together, let us see what he can do.'

'If we want to have the problem solved legally, it will take a long time.'

'Have these Lambadas cultivated the lands legally?'

'They have become foolishly bold by listening to all and sundry.'

'It is not whosoever. It is that teacher's advice. Rather than teach, he does such useless things.'

'We should act in such a way that these Lambadas should not take up the matter of the grazing grounds again. They have to come and surrender here immediately, abandoning their harvest and the grazing grounds.'

'We should see that they have no means of livelihood other than working on our fields.'

It was left to Gowda's discretion to decide what to do and when. Gowda got ready to fulfil the responsibility assigned to him.

Eighteen

The postman who came riding a bicycle from Kalluru came to the school and handed over to me a letter addressed to Somalya. Sometimes the postman would send letters through people who were coming to the Thanda from Kalluru. I went to Somalya's house in the evening with the letter. He not only knew how to sign his name but also tried to read slowly by putting together the letters of the alphabet. Since I was there, he asked me to read the letter for him.

It was from his elder son, Hari. He had decided to marry the daughter of Bhim Singh, who had got him a job. The wedding would be solemnized the following week in Srinidhi Kalyana Mantapam in Vijayapura. Somalya fumed with anger. It hurt him deeply to know that his son had decided to marry without consulting him, and had asked him to attend the wedding in that manner. He shouted, 'Does he not have the time to at least come and talk to us?' Somalaya had wished to see his son's marriage celebrated in a grand manner in the Thanda. 'What sort of wedding is it, if it is arranged in some Kalyana Mantap in a city? Let him get married. Why does he need us at his wedding?' He was very upset.

'Things keep changing with time,' I said.

'It is not like that, master. Our son has become a hostage to our sambandis (in-laws) for a job. Let him get married with none of us – his parents, friends and relatives – attending it.'

'Look here, you were ready to give your daughter in marriage to an old man as his second wife, just because he was rich! Did you not concede to have Rukki married to Lachamya from the village? You agreed because Lachamya had some land. Now, what is wrong with Hari agreeing to the marriage because of the job they got him?'

'I agreed to Rukki's marriage as I'd no choice. Otherwise, her mother would have dragged her into her own business of prostitution. When the boy, girl and girl's mother agreed, I'd no option but to agree. I've already admitted that I was a little hasty in my daughter's case.'

'Don't be hasty in your son's case as well,' I warned him.

Ruplibai, who was listening to our conversation, said, 'Please tell him, master. Wherever they are, if the children are safe and happy we should also be happy. Would it not be wrong to not go to the wedding ceremony? We will lose our son forever and have to spend the rest of our days without him. It would be better to go, even if just as visitors.'

As the wedding day approached, the tension in the atmosphere intensified. Loku was also unhappy with this sudden announcement. He joined his father in being adamant. Ramji, Kasanu's father, supported them, saying, 'The boy should not have done this.' But Kasanu and I argued against this and tried to convince Somalya to change his mind. At last, Ruplibai took to fasting and fought with her adamant husband, who had no option but to relent and agree to attend the wedding. I said, 'I cannot leave the school unattended. You attend.' I bid them farewell.

A thoroughly disappointed group returned from the wedding. Somalya was aghast. 'What kind of wedding was that?' he exclaimed. 'They did not observe any of our rituals. The sambandis did not even speak to us properly. All the women there were draped in silk saris and blouses, master. Our women were wearing skirts, blouses and veils. Believe us, we were like fish out of water in that place. The influence of city fashions and the arrogance of money were quite evident. We were just like dirt under their feet. Don't we have self-respect? What sort of life is it, if one has to live with no self-respect? How well we celebrated the wedding of our Limbya! We celebrated the wedding for four-five days in moonlight and enjoyed ourselves. We spent just a quarter of the money these people had spent lavishly in a single day, and celebrated by dancing and singing in the moonlight instead of sacrificing our customs and rituals. If we lose what we have and imitate others, how does that help us?' Somalya's displeasure found expression in bouts of angry outbursts.

Ruplibai also pulled a long face. She joined her husband in complaining. 'In short, it is like having given birth to the son and looking after him till he grew up, only to be sold out.' She felt the loss of her son very strongly. Loku said, 'Brother and sister-in-law were seated in chairs fit for kings and queens. Well-dressed people came to the wedding on scooters and in cars. There were chairs for everyone to sit on, there was the fragrance of scent, film songs on discs, everything one could ask for, but...'

'Where were our traditional songs? The bride and the groom were shamelessly talking to each other as they were seated, master,' wailed Ruplibai. I kept quiet, not knowing what to say.

❖

The Thanda was on the threshold of a harvest. Rather than work as labourers for the villagers, as was their practice every year, this year they were in a celebratory mood, ready to harvest their own crops. The well-tended land responded generously, with timely rains. The grazing grounds, once full of stones and thorny bushes, had now acquired new life with the living touch of the Lambadas.

One evening, when I was out for a walk, I decided to go towards the grazing grounds. As I stood in the midst the crops, I began to feel the cool, fragrant breeze that was blowing over the crops. It was a pleasure to touch the stalks and ripe ears of corn as I walked.

As I was walking towards the boundary of the grounds, Somalya was absorbed in preparing his choota. He opened the bag, brought out the choota and blew into it. Then he crushed tobacco and filled it in the choota. He then held it between his toes and lit it by striking firestones. He covered it with both his palms, drew a long puff and blew out the smoke, gazing into the sky. Though I went and stood beside him, he did not notice me. I broke his reverie by saying, 'You must be feeling very happy to see the full grown crops.'

'Oh! I didn't see you coming! This land is the gift of Lord Sevalal. Our dream of mother earth has been realized. She is mitigating all our woes. This hillock, this lake, this stream, this land, the cattle that roam around here – this is where I grew up. After acquiring the grazing grounds, we feel luck has opened its doors for us. It may take another four to six days to reap the jowar crop. If the rains fail, if we can continue to grow the crops with the water in the lake, we are sure to get rid of our poverty. Sit down, master. Hope you are not in a hurry?'

'I am out on a leisurely stroll. There is no hurry,' I said, sitting down comfortably. He drew long puffs on the choota and blew out smoke from his nostrils and mouth as he began to speak.

'I am reminded of the harvests of the past. Long ago, Kalluru had suffered a drought. Even back then, people had to leave their homes to go and work as labourers. In the entire village, only a few rich families had managed to stock food in their granaries and could afford to stay back. The rest had to leave in search for work. Working as migratory labourers is not new to us. We had to go to distant places. After crossing Nagarkote, we reached Rajooru for the harvest. Though it did not rain much, the crops were ready after a few showers. They were fertile lands. We divided ourselves into teams of twenty and began to reap the jowar crops. We stayed in the fields outside the village. Hari was a little boy then. After him, we had two sons who did not survive. When we went to harvest the crops, Mariyamma played with our lives. Rupli prayed to the goddess, "Save my children, I will sacrifice a cock, mother." But the goddess seemed to have different designs. The children did not survive. Hari, the lone surviving child, became our darling. He was a very loving child among us. After a few years, Loku and Zimri were born. The depressed Rupli recovered.

'When we went for harvest as labourers we ran into a lot of trouble. When Hari was down with high fever we suffered a lot!

'I was supervising the work of four teams and was also the leader of one team. As we were working in the fields, I would assign a plot to each team and instil a spirit of competition in them. Our people work hard, as if they are possessed. A bag full of jowar was given as wages for reaping one plot of land. While almost everyone was engaged in work, there were a couple of people who would play truant. When complaints of this reached me, I would fine them a paisa. If they did not pay the fine, I would threaten to expel them from our settlement. When threatened like this, they would mend their ways and start working with zeal. I was considerate of those who had a fever or were tired. "Not all fingers are equal. We have to adjust," is what I used to say. When our women sang and men joked as we worked, we never felt the stress and strain of work.

'It must have been three in the afternoon. We had finished our work for the day and had returned to the settlement. On the way back from work, our women carried bundles of green grass for the cattle, while the men drove the cattle, carrying the equipment with them. After returning from work, I would bathe in the open, and Rupli would come and massage my back. We would get busy after returning from work; take a bath, wash clothes, light the stove and make rotis.

'The child Hari who was sleeping, suddenly began to yell and cry loudly. Rupli stopped massaging my back, muttering, "What happened to this lout?" She went over to the crying child and immediately called out to me, frightened. I quickly finished my bath and went over to Hari and touched his body; it was burning like hot coal. When we examined him, we found a lump in the groin region. We had been busy the entire day and couldn't pay him much attention. He had been curled up all day. I did not know why. He began to cry, saying it was aching. Ruplibai felt distressed. She was worried that she would lose another son as well. She prayed to the goddess and made a promise – "Saathi Bhavani yaadi, thon saath kukado bet doochoo (Mother Bhavani, I shall sacrifice seven cocks for you). Please cure my son soon." I prayed to Mariyamma as well and promised to sacrifice a ram in her honour. Rupli firmly believed that this was an expression of the goddess's anger. She took a pinch of ash from the stove and praying to the Mother Goddess, smeared it on the child's forehead.

'At the sound of Rupli's wails, all our people began to gather around our hut. Kasanu's mother and father said, "We did not even realize something was wrong. We thought he was just sleeping since morning." The old woman got a piece of turmeric and ground it on a stone, but the boy would not allow her to apply the paste on him. Kasanu and I had to hold him down firmly. Another woman warmed a piece of cloth on a hot pan and fomented him with it. Everyone tried a different remedy. The two of us made vows to the goddess. The thought of going to a clinic occurred to me and I shared it with Kasanu. He said, "Yes, that is the right thing to do." We took the boy to a doctor in Rajooru. He gave him an injection and said, "Take him to the government hospital in Nagarkote in the morning. He may require surgery." We paid the doctor and brought the boy back. He had by now stopped crying and fallen asleep.

'An operation would cost a lot. I began to worry about how to get so much money. Finally, I thought of asking Yankareddy, who we were working for at the time, and reached his door. It looked more like the gate of a fortress. I called out, "Master, master!" The landlord was making entries in his accounts book. When he heard me he removed his spectacles and came out and asked, "Why have you come at this hour?" I told him everything in detail. "I have to take my son to the government hospital in Nagarkote early in the morning. If you give me five hundred rupees, I shall work hard and repay the money."

'"It's all right. I shall lend you money. You know very well, I don't levy heavy interest like others. Once the harvest is over, you may sell jowar and repay the money or give it back when it is convenient to you." The generous landlord went into the house and came back with five hundred rupees from his chest and counted it three times before giving it to me.

'We reached Nagarkote in a cart early in the morning. We registered our case in the government hospital and sat in the queue waiting for our turn. It was afternoon by the time we could see the doctor. He examined the boy and said, "He has to be operated upon immediately. It will cost five hundred rupees." Though we had five hundred rupees at that time, we knew we would need more money later for medicines and food. I discussed the matter with Kasanu. Both of us together appealed to the doctor to charge us a lower amount. "We can only pay four hundred. Please perform the surgery and save the boy, sir."

'"Do you think you are buying brinjals and onions, that you can bargain? I shall operate only if the full amount is paid," he said. He instructed the nurse to ask us to leave. I thought it would be better to let the future take care of itself. I paid the entire amount and prostrated myself in front of the doctor. As soon as he got the money, his behaviour changed. He asked the nurse to put the boy on a bed, and he promised to operate that night. Kasanu said, "I shall arrange for some more money," and left the place.

'The doctor did not perform the operation that night. My son continued to suffer. The next morning, the young boy who was on the cot next to our son was operated upon. But the boy died during the operation. We were shocked. His mother and father were crying. That boy had been talking to us all through the previous night. His parents had shared the food in their basket with us. Our eyes were filled with tears. We wondered what was writ in the fate of our son. In the afternoon, the doctor was on his rounds visiting the patients and came to examine our son. My wife held on to the doctor's feet – which had shoes on them – and pleaded in a piteous tone, "Please sir, treat our son soon and earn divine blessings by curing him."

'"Che, che, let me go, let me go," he said, wringing himself free and walking away. The nurse scolded Rupli and asked her to keep quiet. At last, the boy was operated upon. Kasanu sold two goats and brought more money. I can never forget the way he helped us as a friend. Hari began to get better. But, how horrible! The stench in that hospital was unbearable! We could not eat anything while we were there. We should never ever fall ill and go to hospitals, don't you agree? God should not make us become victims of a doctor...Whatever it may be, the boy survived. The doctor retained the boy for five days and then discharged him from the hospital. Mariyamma and Sevabhai blessed us.

'We have suffered like this to save our son, master. The son is educated and has got a job now. We are all proud of him. But after having tended him all these years, it is as if some vulture has snatched him away from us. He neither sought our permission nor informed us, but got married all of a sudden. And what sort of marriage was it? It was a marriage of convenience, like a marriage of jackals. Was this marriage according to our customs? We wanted to perform the marriage in moonlit nights in a grand manner that the people of the Thanda would remember for a long time. We were meek like sheep in this city marriage. My wife is more disturbed than I am.'

As he spoke, his eyes became moist with tears. I tried to console him. 'Nothing untoward has happened. Why do you worry unnecessarily? How can he forget you? You have brought him up, sent him to school, he has come up in his life.'

'Che. He has married without asking us, married without seeking the blessings of the gods in the Thanda. I don't feel all right. I have no peace of mind. As a matter of duty I attended the marriage and blessed him, that's all.'

'Don't worry about all that now. There is a bountiful crop before you. How do you feel about that?' I said, in an attempt to divert his attention.

'This has given us a lot of pleasure. This has been a realization of our dream. We have to get ready now to pull out the jowar. There won't be any time to rest once the harvest begins till the crop reaches home,' he said.

I sensed his mood change a bit. 'Would you like to sit here a little longer?' I asked. 'You may go. I shall sit a little longer and come,' he said.

Nineteen

The people of the Thanda, who went to work as labourers in the farms of the villagers during each harvesting season in the past, began to reap their own crops this year. They got up early in the morning at four to reap the jowar and worked till around one in the afternoon. Thereafter, they returned home, bathed, and rested in the yard of Sevalal's temple or under the shade of the neem tree. One evening, around seven, a boy came running and announced, 'Four to six heads of cattle had entered the fields, and I drove them away.' Somalya sent a few of the youngsters to the field to look into the matter. Around eight in the night there was news of large herds of cattle having entered the fields. 'Kalluru people have let a large herd of cattle into the field; come in large numbers, all of you come, come fast,' shouted someone from the direction of the fields. Startled, Somalya, Kasanu, Damla, Loku, Dhenya and others rushed towards the fields, staves in their hands.

Other than setting hundreds of cattle on the fields, a few men had also entered the fields and cut the ears of the jowar crop. The people of the Thanda rushed into the field to drive the cattle away. The cows began to moo and run helter skelter. The people of Kalluru, who were hiding, suddenly began to attack us with their staves. It was difficult to recognize who they were in the dim moonlight. On behalf of all the landlords, Gowda seemed to have sent a large number of pariahs and hunters after making them

drink to their fill. Stones and staves flew all over the fields. My heart was filled with fear at the commotion.

Only the aged, children and women had remained in the Thanda. The women came out of their huts and started shouting at the people of Kalluru. A few women started running towards the fields, worried about their menfolk. Meanwhile, some goondas from Kalluru entered the Thanda with staves in their hands. When the women and children began to wail and cry, Duglibai, Ruplibai, Lalibai and a few other women took some sticks and pestles and stood guard. I appealed to the villagers, 'I beseech you with folded hands, don't fight. Why do you want to attack women and children? If you feel you have been met with injustice, go to the police station and lodge a complaint.'

Nobody was prepared to listen to me. One of them grabbed me and said, 'Eh, master, you have grown too big for your boots. If you want to do your job properly, do it. Why do you interfere in our affairs?' Another fellow came forward and thrashed me with a stick, dragged me to the school, pushed me inside, latched the door and went away. I lay there, moaning in pain. I recovered in a short while and started gazing out of the window. In the dim moonlight it was difficult to make out who was thrashing who. I could hear the sound of fighting, swearing and shouting. Duglibai had locked the girls in Sevabhai's temple and stood guard at the door with a pestle in hand. Ruplibai, Lalibai and others started shouting as if they were possessed by devils and kept the miscreants at bay. The older people were appealing piteously, 'Leave us alone, what has prompted you to behave like this, what wrong have we committed?'

Four to six villagers somehow managed to sneak in from behind and set the bullocks and sheep free and started beating them. A couple of them abducted Duglibai. Each one of them was completely drunk. Two of them held her hands, and two others pinned down her legs and then took turns to rape her. She cried like a lamb caught in the jaws of a wolf. Though all this happened to her, the rest did not seem to have noticed this.

Though the Thanda people were successful in driving the Kalluru people away, they had been badly injured. Somalya put to test his skills of wrestling, which he had acquired earlier, and drove a few people away. But at some point during the fight, someone attacked him from behind and hit him hard on his head with a stick. Blood began to flow from his head. Kasanu's kneecaps were damaged, leaving him in unbearable pain. When the two of them were being carried to the Thanda, the goondas who had entered the Thanda set fire to the huts. When Ruplibai began to chase them with a burning piece of bamboo in her hand, her hair dishevelled, they dispersed quickly as if they were being chased by the devil. When no one could be caught, she began to shout, 'If we want to cultivate our own lands and live without being dependent on others, do you want to destroy us? Do you want to make us homeless by setting our roofs on fire? Come, you bastards, come!'

Meanwhile, everyone tried to put out the fire by throwing mud and water on the flames. Once the roofs burnt away, the supporting pillars stood stark naked. Some attended to Somalya and Kasanu. Ruplibai, who returned to the Thanda after throwing away the piece of bamboo, saw Somalya unconscious and began to cry loudly. Though Loku told his mother, 'Nothing has happened, he is just unconscious, keep quiet,' she continued to wail. She bandaged his bleeding head with her veil and started massaging his hands and legs. When he finally came to and let out a moan, life seemed to return to her.

As people gradually started gathering at the platform under the neem tree after recovering a little from the wounds they had received, I began to bang on the doors of the school loudly. Loku came and opened the door. When he saw my torn shirt and swollen face in the lamp light, he said, 'They have done a lot of damage, master.' I made enquiries about everyone. 'Right now, everyone is just lying down. Let's not talk now; let's talk in the morning,' replied Loku. I went out, eased myself and went back into the room to lie down. I fell asleep after a while.

The following morning, the Thanda felt like a burial ground. Every face was drained of all blood. Though Somalya had regained consciousness the previous night, he was still drowsy. When I stood in front of him, he did not recognize me. He was talking to himself, 'Sevabhai, all of you guarded the Thanda, but what has been the result? Where are we? That goddess who did not spare even you – how much she made you suffer! Was that not sufficient? Not once or twice – she took away your life! Then what about us? Goddess, there is no end to our suffering, test us to any extent you want, you cannot do this once we are not here, can you?' He was in his own world. Ruplibai began to cry, 'Master, see what our fate is like. In one word, we are not lucky, that's all.' Duglibai, who had appeared to be a strong woman, was reduced to a heap. One look at her, and anyone would be moved to pity and begin to retch. Rukki and Limbya began to treat her. Limbya's body was also swollen.

Kasanu, who was unable to stand up and move, said from where he was seated, 'You have seen our state, master. The school may not function for quite some time, go home. You should not get involved in our troubles and you should not be beaten up either.' The rest also expressed the same opinion. I had never ever thought of leaving the Thanda in this state. I had imagined leaving on a transfer, carrying with me the love and affection of all the people of the prosperous Thanda.

When I reached the school, Thukya, who was under the feudal service of Gowda, was sitting there. He used to come to the Thanda occasionally. His speech was always filled with irony. He was also proud that he was the servant of Gowda. If someone asked, 'Are you keeping well?' his repartee would be 'I am here standing in front of you, because I'm well.' If someone remarked as a matter of courtesy in the morning, 'Are you up already?' he would respond, 'Do I look like someone who is lying

down?' Such was his awkwardness. I wondered why this person, foreboding evil, was here. 'Do you understand, master? We have to know our own limitations. How can the Thanda people think of cultivating their own lands? Those who engage themselves in daydreams come to this fate. We should not rebel against the wealthy and the lords, should we? If we serve them well, we can enjoy all comforts. There are a few people who give heed to all and sundry and lead the Thanda astray. I wonder if they will learn their lesson now.' When he spoke in this manner, I felt the insinuations were directed at me.

I applied for long leave and packed my trunk and left the place. Limbya came to see me off up to the Kalluru crossroad. Though I asked him not to take the trouble as he was badly beaten up, he insisted on coming with me. When we were at the crossroad, some Kalluru people were watching us. I thought they were talking about us.

When I reached Nagarkote and informed Hiralal about what had transpired, there was a quiver in my voice. He sympathized with me for having been beaten up. He said, 'We should not let this matter rest. I shall look into it. For the present, you go home. But you should come back to the school in the Thanda again. I'll take up this fight as a challenge.' So saying, he bid me goodbye.

Though I came home, I was haunted by memories of the Thanda. In a few days, I received orders about my transfer from the Thanda. It is true that government servants get transferred. But the situation and the circumstances under which this transfer took place disturbed me a lot. Though I had been to the Thanda to work as a teacher, I had not confined myself to my job. I had become part of their life, their celebrations and their struggle. While I was waiting for those happy moments when the school would develop and the people would gain ownership of the grazing grounds and become happy, I had to witness their immense pain and suffering. This had disturbed me deeply. Another disturbing factor was the reason assigned for my transfer. I was accused of having instigated the people and getting involved in political activities.

Some people advised me on how to carry on my work and to what extent to get involved in people's affairs. I could not express my intense grief and despair to anyone. 'Whatever the matter, I am glad you got yourself free from the Thanda,' said one of my friends, expressing relief. Though the people in my house were disturbed with the accusation made against me, they were happy that I had got my freedom from the Thanda. But I could not get myself free from the memories of the Thanda, from what happened to Somalya. How far the struggle for the grazing grounds had come!

Part II

Twenty

(Loku is the narrator)

I will narrate what happened after Basappa master left the Thanda. We had not yet resumed our work. One evening, we were all either in our huts, or in front of the Sevalal temple or on the platform under the neem tree. In fact, we were drained of all our energies after this incident. Bapu, in particular, was deeply hurt and saddened. He spent all day just sitting idly perhaps because he was hit on the head or maybe he was in a state of shock. A police van roared into our Thanda. The police entered the Thanda just like the Kalluru people had – with sticks, like wolves entering a herd of sheep. A few policemen went around twirling their batons and making enquiries. Two of them had rifles. 'Who are the people who attacked the people of the village? All of you get into the van quickly,' ordered a policeman.

'We did not attack them, they attacked us and burnt down our huts,' I began to say.

'He talks too much. Kick him and put him in first,' ordered the havaldar.

'Why?' I asked.

'You want to know why you are being arrested, do you. You bastard, you have grown too big for your boots. Get into the van first,' he barked, putting his hand on my behind and pushing me into the vehicle. The rest of the police went around the Thanda and shoved my father, mother, Kasanu, Damla, Khubya, Duglibai, Rukki, Limbya and others – around fifteen of us – into the van. 'My father is not well, please leave him,' I requested. But my cries fell on deaf ears. After taking us to the Nagarkote police station, they wrote down our names and pushed us into the lockup.

When Hiralal learnt that we had been brought in for interrogation and thrown into jail, he wrote a letter to the higher authorities in the police department. As a result, a few people from Kalluru were also arrested and put in a different cell. Arresting them was mere eyewash. In fact, the police had connived with the people of the village.

They began to question us one by one, beating us so hard on our elbows and knees that we shrieked in pain. 'You bastards,' screamed the policemen as they beat us. 'You have become arrogant. You don't want to attend to the work in the fields of the Kalluru landlords! Do you want to till the lands illegally?' Those giant policemen beat us with each utterance. Though we pleaded saying, 'We are not at fault; we are not the ones who attacked; we had to fight to protect ourselves,' they did not listen to us. Instead, they went on battering us and shouting at us. I don't think father was beaten very hard in the cell. He was already subdued. Still, he must have received a few blows. He had even stopped eating the food provided to him in the jail. He would have a couple of morsels when he was coaxed. When he was made to stand in the dock in the court, he began to cry. He had suffered a lot. He was choked with the thought that he, who was dispensing justice in the Thanda, had to stand here in the dock as a criminal. I thought father was losing his courage and self-confidence as he grew old.

Hiralal got into an argument with the police officials. 'You have unnecessarily arrested them and are torturing the innocent. What is wrong if one fights to protect oneself?' The officer countered, 'Has that land been registered in their names? If it was a registered land, I would have myself asked them to cultivate the land. Is it not illegal to use the grazing grounds for agriculture?

If the people of the village let their cattle graze in the grazing grounds, what is wrong with that?' After a lot of tussle, Hiralal was able to have us released on bail. The people of the village had already been released on bail on a surety given by Gowda.

Hari is also said to have attempted to have us released using his father-in-law's influence. A day after we were released and returned to the thanda, Hari came from Vijayapura. Father was very weak. He was in his obsessions. Kasanu called Hari and said, 'You take your father with you. He is very upset. It could be because of the injury on his head. Have him examined by a good doctor there. Let your mother also come with you. Let the two of them get some rest there.' Hari told him that he was also thinking on similar lines. Father and mother left the Thanda most unwillingly. Hari had arranged for a vehicle.

The whole Thanda had gathered to bid them good-bye. People talked among themselves, 'Our Nayak is a blessed person. His son is educated and has a good job. Now both of them will be with the elder son in a city and live happily. They must have sought this boon from Sevalal.' I also thought father would receive good medical attention and stay in comfort in Vijayapura, but after they left, the house felt desolate. The entire Thanda respected my brother Hari for his decision. He had money. Besides, he had spent money liberally here in our Thanda. Therefore, everyone in the Thanda praised him wholeheartedly. What if I am not as well educated as he is? I shall earn more money than he does and be recognized as a respectable man. This thought became firm within me.

In a way it was good that father left the Thanda. This is because as long as he was around, I could not exert my authority. I had to seek his permission for everything. If he objected to something, it would just not be done. What he said was gospel. Where was the freedom to act as I wished? I had appreciated the efforts he had put in to earn a status for the Thanda. But he had unnecessarily objected to the marriage of my younger sister.

What was the need to have Rukki's marriage performed with pomp? He was blinded by the thought of developing the Thanda and never thought of developing himself or his family. As the saying goes, 'no community acknowledges your service, nor does a cadaver appreciate all the makeup.'

After the fight that took place between the village and the Thanda, I tried to make peace. As we had settled beside the village, I tried to convince our people to not offend the villagers. After coming back from the police station, both the villagers and the people of the Thanda had cooled down. I convened a meeting of the villagers, including their youngsters, and the youngsters from the Thanda with the help of Thukya, Gowda's servant. I appealed with folded hands, 'We have always worked together. Why should there be discord between us now? We shall come to you as labourers when we are free. If we cannot come, we shall help you connect with our people in other settlements. Do not worry about harvesting your crops. We shall be responsible for it. Right?'

The village youngsters agreed to this. Everyone blamed Gowda and Setty. Though a lot of crop was damaged, we salvaged what was left. We could gather enough food grain to last us for five to six months. Because of my role in brokering peace, my contacts in the village increased. In a few days, the panchayat elections were held. Many young people from the village had contested. Since one seat was reserved for the Thanda, my name was proposed unanimously.

As I became a member of the panchayat, I gained respect both in the town and in the Thanda. Naturally, the importance of the elders in the Thanda was ebbing. Whenever there was a major dispute, people of the Thanda were summoned to the Kalluru panchayat. Our elders tried to force their opinion. 'Disputes of the Thanda are best settled here with our elders rather than taking it to the Kalluru panchayat,' they said. I countered, saying, 'I have no objection. But under the changed circumstances, when

problems are acute, there is nothing wrong in taking our people there.'

There was a scheme – the Janata Housing Scheme – to build free houses for the poor. President Ningappa of the panchayat suggested that some houses could be allotted to the Thanda as part of this scheme. 'Though they are supposed to be free of cost, we need to take some money. Let this be between us. You retain your share and give me the rest of the money,' he said. I began to negotiate with people in the Thanda who needed a house. It was essential for me to be practical. In the meantime, I also had my own house renovated. I got a commission from the contractor when the Janata houses were built. Fifteen houses were somehow built in the first instalment of the free housing scheme.

Since I began to prosper financially, my people began to feel jealous of me. We were able to harvest two crops from the grazing grounds in two years. A majority of the people were saved from starvation. Besides, everyone was charged with a newfound purpose in life.

If this had continued there would have been no trouble. But there was a sense of discomfort among the people of Kalluru. Some of them had approached Venkanna Desai who had settled in Mumbai and were pestering him, saying, 'You hold the ownership of the grazing grounds, please take possession of it.' We were filled with fear. What would happen if action was taken to implement this suggestion? I kept thinking of what the police officer had asked me earlier. 'Have these grazing lands been registered in your names?' I decided if the lands get registered in our names, a major worry would be put to rest. I met Hiralal and told him, 'We should not keep quiet and become complacent as we are cultivating the lands now. The behaviour of the villagers changes often like the colours of a chameleon.' Though an appeal had already been made to the minister requesting him to settle the matter related to the grazing grounds favourably, no action had been taken yet.

Together, we went to meet the district collector. But the district collector we had appealed to had been transferred. We apprised the new district collector about the matter in detail. He sent us back saying, 'I have to look into the files. I cannot make a hasty decision. You may come back in a week's time.' We also met the concerned clerk and bribed him adequately to ensure that the file was placed on the officer's desk for his perusal. He assured us that in a week's time he would certainly have the file processed. We went there exactly in a week's time. We met the clerk, who told us, 'The file is already on the officer's desk. Please go and meet him.' Accordingly, we went in and stood in front of the officer. He did not look at us till he had settled two or three cases on hand. Afterwards, he looked at us askance. Once again, we recounted our woes.

He turned over the pages of the file and brought up the matter of the Kalluru people having made an application. 'Lambadas have been cultivating the lands unauthorizedly; it is also a piece of land irrigated by the lake water,' he read out from the file. He looked up from the file and told us, 'You need to write to the Minor Irrigation Projects Department. Once we receive an approval from them, further course of action will be easy.' He suggested that we go and meet the minister of Minor Irrigations.

The political scenario had been through some significant changes since we had first made our application regarding the grazing grounds. You know we had all been to the speech given by the minister named Puttappa along with Basappa master. The young man, Jagadish, who belonged to the party of the minister had come to us and pleaded, 'We need a youngster from among you to be a member of the panchayat. But all of you should support us during the elections.' Our people had suggested my name. Jagadish, who had made several promises, was not to be found at the time of minister's speech. This Jagadish came to the Thanda after several days. 'I could not be with you all at the time of minister's speech. This is because the minister had sent me to attend to some of his personal work. Once again, it is he who has sent me here today.'

Elections for the Legislative Assembly were announced. As per our agreement, we supported Puttappa. We also saw to it that his opponent, Siddappa, was not allowed to canvass in the Thanda. But Puttappa's money, power and other tactics did not yield results. Siddappa belonged to the upper caste. Several businessmen had financed Siddappa's campaign in the elections. The caste advantage and the power of money helped Siddappa win the elections.

To seek an appointment with the minister of Minor Irrigations, it was necessary to meet Siddappa, who was now the legislator. His endorsement was essential. When Hiralal and I went to meet him he had some choice fiery words for us. 'When we came to the Thanda to canvass, you did not allow us to enter the place. Now you have come to request me to have the grazing grounds registered. How dare you come here now? Go and ask that ex-minister Puttappa to help you. Let me see how this can happen. I will not rest till I teach you people a lesson. All of you are becoming haughty.' Hiralal gathered courage to speak. 'In the elections, people cast their votes without being aware of who they are voting for. But once a person is elected, he is a representative of the people and should not mind these matters and bear a generous attitude towards all.' Hiralal also praised the legislator a little. But even that did not yield any result.

With no option left, we went to the former minister Puttappa and apprised him of the anger expressed by the legislator and asked him to look into the matter. 'The minister of Minor Irrigations may belong to another party, but he is a friend of mine. Don't worry, I shall have the work done,' he said. We met the minister for Minor Irrigations with his letter. He gathered details from the concerned secretary and issued orders to the chief engineer.

I believe the matter of the grazing grounds was discussed in the district committee meeting of the Banjara Association at Nagarkote. A resolution was passed that the expenses to be incurred have to be met by all the members and that Hiralal and I should continue to pursue the matter together. When we went to Bengaluru and enquired with the chief engineer, we learnt that a letter had been sent across to the superintending engineer. Hiralal wrote a letter to the concerned official to expedite the matter. After several days, we learnt that the executive engineer of the division had been instructed to personally inspect the situation and submit a report. Hiralal got busy with matters related to his company during the next two months.

I went to Vijayapura to meet father and mother. When I informed father about the recent developments and the efforts I had put in to resolve the matter, he felt happy. Though he appeared to have recovered, he had lost the cheer and verve he had earlier. Hari bhai had been taking him to a neurologist for consultations once a month. Mother, on the other hand, had developed asthma. They were in no condition to return to the Thanda. But they gathered all the information about the Thanda. They elicited detailed information about everyone from me and felt happy recollecting the days they had spent in the Thanda.

The problem of the grazing grounds became more complicated. Siddappa instigated the people of Kalluru when he learnt that the executive engineer along with the assistant engineer were to visit the place for inspection. A day before their scheduled visit to the contested grounds, the people of Kalluru broke the bund on the tank and let the water flow into the fields. They also diverted the water from the canals into the fields. When the executive engineer visited the grazing grounds the following day, the whole place was inundated with water. He came to the conclusion that the whole area was part of the lake. The people of the Thanda hurriedly went to the fields and explained the situation to him. 'We grow our crops here. It is true that right now it looks like there are no crops here. But if you properly examine the place, you will understand. The people of Kalluru have released water into the fields.' They appealed to the engineer fervently. But the engineer was curt, 'I don't know anything about these matters. I shall report what I have seen at the time of my visit.'

All of this transpired during my visit to Vijayapura. Encouraged by this, the people of Kalluru once again became aggressive and quarrelsome with us. The government made an announcement that the entire area was part of the tank and could not be allotted to the Lambadas.

Hiralal got in touch with a lawyer who was fighting for the welfare of the nomads and the tribal people and apprised him of the matter. There was a positive response from him. Our problem was taken to court.

In the meantime, our people started going back to work as labourers. Some immigrated to towns to seek jobs. It became obligatory on our part to work on farms in Kalluru and other villages during harvest season. The illicit liquor trade flourished unabashedly in the Thanda. Though several small houses were built to provide living spaces, the question of food and sustenance loomed large.

The lawyer took up our problem of the grazing grounds and argued in court on the basis of the commitments made by the government as well as witnesses and won the case on our behalf. The police came and warned the people of Kalluru not to interfere in matters of the cultivation of the grazing grounds. The people of Kalluru said, 'We will no longer listen to that legislator Siddappa, you may put the grazing grounds to use.' There was a reason behind this change of tune. By now, the legislator had become extremely arrogant. Some of the residents of Kalluru were also disgusted with him. He had favoured the people of his caste and neglected the others; he extracted money from people with assurance of getting their work done but did not honour his commitment. Such behaviour was revolting to the villagers. Thus, there was no resistance from the people of Kalluru, at least for the present.

I gathered the important people of the Thanda and discussed the possibilities of cultivating the land again. By now, they had lost interest in cultivation. They were not as enthusiastic as earlier. Nevertheless, I persisted, mentioning that it was not appropriate to neglect the land when it was in our possession. They said, 'Let's not cultivate as a group any more. Divide the lands and give us our share.' We divided the lands accordingly. We went to Nagarkote and got the lands registered in our names. Hiralal and Ningappa, the president of the Kalluru panchayat, helped us in the task. There was a sense of relief.

I wrote a letter to my brother in Vijayapura about the registration of the grazing grounds. He wrote back in reply, 'Father is very happy to receive this news. But his behaviour has been strange. Mother's asthma has aggravated. Please come here at the earliest.'

I assigned the work of repairing the bund on the lake to some workers and left for Vijayapura. My brother was full of complaints about father and mother. I believe, once the two of them were so upset with him that they packed their bags and went up to the bus stand. He brought them back. He also gave me an account of the amount of money he had spent on looking after them. All said, father was immensely happy that the lands now legally belonged to us. He shared his thoughts on how to cultivate these lands and what crops to grow there.

'We should do everything at the right time. We are now in good times. We need not worry now. Troubled times for our people have come to an end. Our Thanda is a good place, it's a sanctified place, a golden land. I've been there since my childhood; I've wandered around the place, I've worked there and while tending cattle I've tasted the fruits and berries growing in the plants.' He ruminated about his past while expressing his satisfaction. While talking about mother's asthma, he said, 'Look, sometimes she behaves as if she is going to breathe her last.' Mother made me sit beside her and said, 'We will come to the Thanda. There is no dearth of food and drink here. Your brother looks after us very well, but somehow we feel imprisoned. Don't say this to your brother. Taking these medicines, visiting the doctor and taking injections – I am tired of all this.'

'Where will we find a doctor in our place, if there are health problems? So stay here. You may come back once you get well. Besides, father has to consult the doctor regularly,' I said.

'If I can perform your marriage and die, I'll be happy,' she said.

'Don't speak of such things. Just keep quiet.' I told her. Her eyes filled with tears.

We got busy with repairing the lake and preparing the fields for cultivation. One day, all of a sudden, a car came at full speed and stopped in front of our house. I went out to see who it could be. Venkanna, Kalluru Desai's son who lives in Mumbai, and Ningappa, president of the Kalluru panchayat, got down from the car and walked into the house. I made some tea on the stove and brought it for them. Mr Desai began, 'Loku, I hear you have become a member of the panchayat. Good, good! I'm glad you people have begun to progress these days. You're getting educated. All this is okay, but you are yet to prosper economically. You must have heard about my grandfather who looked after your people and the facilities he offered them in the good old days! Now I have come with a proposal of a welfare scheme for you. Some time back, several people had told me that the grazing grounds belonged to my grandfather and the Lambadas are cultivating it now. I did not pay any heed to it. Anyway, the court has now given its decision in your favour. The grazing grounds are registered in your names. That settles the matter. Nobody can raise any objection. Right now, I plan to start a company. I would like you to be its manager and look after it.' I was totally confused. 'I have barely got through my matriculation. I don't have much knowledge; besides, I don't know what your company does, how can I agree to this?'

'The rocks on the hillocks surrounding the Thanda attached to Kalluru are of very good quality. I learnt this recently. Wonderful granite stones. Export quality stones can be extracted. These days it is not easy to take to farming as it was in earlier times. Fertilizers, pesticides, everything has become expensive. After all this, when the crops are ready, we may not get a good price. So, I propose to buy these grazing grounds from you. I shall pay a good price for every acre. Your people can use this as seed money and engage in different trades. Otherwise, they can work in our company as stone crushers and loaders or take up small contracts. I have decided to make you the manager. I shall pay you ten thousand rupees a month as salary. Depending on the profits, I may increase it.'

'Just accept it,' said Ningappa. 'I'm also giving away my fields to these people. Granite has been found there as well.' He then took me outside and whispered in my ear, 'Venkanna Desai is a very nice man. He has never claimed his rights over the lands owned by his forefathers. Now he is giving you a fair price. Even the government is not likely to give such rich compensation for areas that will be submerged. Besides, you will be the manager of the company. Many of your people will also get employment. Think it over!' I thought this was an acceptable proposal and consented with a nod of my head. The two of them said many other things. I told them, 'I like your proposal. I shall talk to my people and let you know their decision.'

'Let us know in a week's time. Lot of work needs to be done urgently,' Venkanna Desai said.

I mulled over the matter after Ningappa and Mr Desai left. There was truth in what they said. With great difficulty, we had gained possession of the lands after fighting for it in the court. Once again, we are going to lose it. But they are not snatching it away from us! They are paying a price, which is not offered in any of the surrounding areas, stretching across ten leagues. Who would pay so much money? If we sell our land, which has been broken into small pieces, to any outsider, can it fetch such a handsome price? What guarantee is there that the people of Kalluru will not trouble us once again? It's almost impossible for anyone to pay as much as Mr Desai has offered us. A manager's job for me, a pay packet of ten thousand rupees. I might surpass my brother Hari in my earnings. Long ago, I had boasted in the presence of Basappa master, 'Watch out, someday I shall earn more than Hari.' Now I have got an opportunity to make that happen. I have to utilize it properly. I have to see to it that our people agree to this proposal. My mind was made up.

After I became a member of the Kalluru panchayat, Thukya, the trusted servant of Gowda, became close to me. He would meet me every time I went to the panchayat office. Though he was a weird person, of late he had been speaking to me affectionately.

However, he was always critical of both Kasanu and father and held them responsible for all the damage done to the Thanda. Since he had helped me patch up the misunderstandings between the Thanda and Kalluru, I tried to use his help to win over the people of the Thanda regarding the sale of the grazing grounds. He suggested that we take people who are likely to agree with us into confidence first, and later approach the rest. I had often heard Damla say, 'I am fed up with this Thanda. If I get a few thousand rupees, I plan to go away to Mangalore or Goa with my family.' I thought if I could win him over, that would strengthen my case. All said, he was a frank and outspoken person. He would put forth his point of view firmly and argue forcefully. Thukya tried to take the outspoken Damla into confidence.

I floated an opinion among the people that it would be wise to reap the benefits available now and liberate ourselves from the grazing grounds, which had already caused us enough trouble. When I was confident that many people would support me, I called for a meeting. Kasanu, Limbya and Khubya might oppose me, I was afraid. I address Kasanu as uncle. I address his father Ramji as granddad. Kasanu was a simple man, but he would never swerve from his principles. He was not a fair weather person.

A meeting was convened. There were arguments and counter-arguments. I explained the issues. I tried to convince everyone that it would be wise to take advantage of the present situation and benefit from it. 'We're not destined to possess lands. It is not that you are not aware of the struggle we had to put up with. We have had several bitter fights and losses. Mr Desai has come with an offer which no other landlord is prepared to pay. This will be the most profitable transaction for us. Though the fields may be ours forever, cultivating them is not a simple task. We need to struggle in the fields! We need to wait for the rains for the lake to get filled. We need to use fertilizers. We need to invest money every year. If we accept Mr Desai's offer, we will earn much more than the wages we earn as labourers. A job in a stone quarry is a job with a very good salary.' A large number of people, especially the youth, supported my point of view. Damla began to dance. As expected, the major opposition came from Kasanu. I asked him, 'Kasanu uncle, there was a time when possessing fields was considered a major achievement. Now it is not so. Times are changing, the world is progressing. In times such as this, what is the point hankering after lands and fields?'

In response, Kasanu said, 'Yes, but can we eat stones? If you sow seeds in the earth, it bears fruit. If mother earth is pleased, we can feed ourselves. Don't fall prey to money. Think of the future. The land is fertile, let us grow crops.' We were not able to take a decision that day. Kasanu and his supporters went to meet Hiralal who had put in a lot of effort to get us the grazing grounds. He apparently said, 'It's true that we fought for the lands. We won it with the intervention of the court. My objective was to see that our Lambadas prosper. Now Mr Desai is offering a price far higher than what others are prepared to pay. Just accept it. If you want lands, acquire them elsewhere without spending this money. I have also discussed the matter with all of them. Just accept it.' Kasanu and the others with him were a little taken aback at his response. According to the information I got, Mr Desai had already given Hiralal one lakh rupees and asked him to help settle the matter of the grazing grounds in his favour without any protest or strike. Hiralal must have agreed to this.

In about a week's time, Mr Desai came and distributed money among all of us. Kasanu and his friends accepted the money without a murmur. They also stopped talking to me. Though I had worked for the welfare and benefit of everyone, they did not understand my good intentions. They began to accuse me of being an unworthy son of a worthy father. Though I had always respected Kasanu, addressing him as uncle, he began to speak ill of me. The bonds that existed between the two families began to weaken.

They did not understand that we would be left far behind in this fast moving world if we followed in the footsteps of my father. They did not appreciate my progressive ideas. Acquiring lands and engaging in agriculture reflected values and ambitions possessed by father and Kasanu. Following this path of farming may provide some money for food and clothing. But when would we liberate ourselves and become wealthy people? For me, sky is the limit. But my people have limited wants. That's why they have still not been able to climb a tall ladder. Father is like a frog in the well. He is not aware of the rivers and the seas. We have a great opportunity now to escape our present insecure state. We should climb higher and higher without looking down.

Until recently, the stillness and silence of a burial ground had prevailed in the Thanda. A lot of activity has now begun since the industrialization! Cranes, trucks and jeeps have arrived. Roads have been laid for their movement. There is celebration and merriment everywhere. Dynamite has begun to explode all over the place. There is noise everywhere. I have started to work as a manager. A house was built for me. Labourers from different places have begun to pour into our Thanda for work. I was attracted to Lachumi, one of the workers who had come to the Thanda and I asked her to do my household chores. Some other girls also came with her. We have struggled for so long. Why should we not enjoy the pleasures of life now? We should enjoy all the comforts and happiness life has to offer to the full.

Mr Desai realized that ruby red and pink stones that are internationally well known are located here, and therefore took up this venture. He has begun to receive a good price for the stones. Mr Desai had tried his hand at various trades while in Mumbai and suffered losses. The goddess Lakshmi is favouring him now. I am supervising the work of blasting the stones and transporting the rocks, while someone who is senior to me is looking after the marketing. Mr Desai's APD Company has begun to earn huge profits.

Mr Desai was impressed by our god Sevalal's temple. He believed that all his prosperity was due to the blessings of this god. Therefore, he built a magnificent temple in his honour. He wanted to instal an idol inside and also perform a havan. When he invited the purohit (priest) in Kalluru to perform the rituals, I am told he behaved rather arrogantly and spurned the offer. Perhaps he was miffed because he was not consulted by Mr Desai when he settled in Mumbai. He did not even seek his guidance after coming back. Or perhaps he was worried that going to the Thanda and performing havan there might not be in accordance with the holy observances followed by orthodox Brahmins. But Mr Desai was not someone to take things lying down. He spent a lot of money and got a purohit from Mumbai to perform the havan. He also rewarded the purohit with generous gifts. The purohit in Kalluru must have felt miserable when he heard about this. Mr Desai also appointed a priest from outside to take care of the daily rituals in the temple. Now there is a prayer ceremony every day at the Sevalal temple with incense, lights and aarthi.

With a new development each day, the Thanda has changed so much that it is difficult to recognize it. This has turned into a world of Kubera, the god of wealth. Two upmarket lodges have been built in Kalluru. Customers from different states and countries come and stay here. Kalluru has not remained the old Kalluru. Different kinds of shops and bars have opened there. They keep their doors open throughout the night, with their colourful lamps glittering in the dark. Factories to polish granite stones have also been established in Kalluru. Finance companies that promise to double the customer's money or sometime multiply it ten times have also been set up. The tinkle of coins and the rustle of crisp currency notes could be heard everywhere. In three years, the face of the Thanda and Kalluru changed completely.

Many of our huts have been converted into houses of brick and cement. Motorcycles and tractors are seen in front of several houses. Our people have begun to visit the brandy shops in

Kalluru for a drink. But our illicit liquor trade continues for the sake of the labourers. Even to this day, some of the residents prefer the liquor brewed in the Thanda to the arrack sold in bottles as it provides a better kick; the country liquor trade has also flourished.

Damla, who had declared that he was fed up with the Thanda, collected his share of the money and left for Goa with his family. His wife and children were not willing. But being bound by affection for him and attracted by the promises he made, they joined him. If he had remained here, he would have been my trusted lieutenant.

Electric lights began to glow in the Thanda at night. Water filled in an overhead tank is supplied to every household through taps. Perhaps, when father gets back to the Thanda, it will have grown beyond his recognition.

A big building has been built for the school now. Three teachers have been appointed. All of them stay in Kalluru and commute to the Thanda for work. They are not like Basappa master who lived amidst us and encouraged our children. In a way, this system is better. This way, they will not get involved in our affairs and create problems. They just do their job and leave.

After becoming the manager, I did not find any time to go to Vijayapura and see my parents. But I was in regular correspondence with Hari. I had informed him about the progress of the Thanda and especially my financial prosperity through my letters. He wrote back saying that since the news of the developments would upset father, he had just told him, 'Everything is all right. They are sowing seeds and growing crops in the grazing grounds.'

Twenty-one

(Zimri is the narrator)

This is a matter from long ago. I had to elope with my uncle Kheera to Goa. Otherwise, it was certain that my father would marry me off to some old hag. Loku, my brother, helped me in this. I need to share yet another secret – I had already conceived at the time and was in the second month of my pregnancy. Kheera and I had already started living as man and wife. Father was not aware of these developments, and even mother was ignorant. Loku had understood and appreciated our love. He knew father would not yield to any appeal as he was adamant and suggested that we get away from the place and settle down in some town. He also planned our elopement. He asked Kheera to reach Nagarkote bus stand and wait for me to join him. I boarded the bus, according to his plan. Father and mother were not home. When they were engaged in farm work on the grazing grounds, Loku and I reached Kalluru bus stand. Though he reassured me as I boarded the bus, I was nervous and my heart throbbed rather fast.

This was the first time I had ever come to Nagarkote bus stand all by myself. When I got off the bus, I was not able to spot Kheera. I broke into a cold sweat with fear. Mother Mariyamma, what shall I do? What would happen if someone spotted me and informed my father? Or, if for some reason, Kheera wouldn't come? My thoughts went astray and I began to feel like a fish out of water. In my anxiety, I wandered around the whole place. Those were some long hours that I had to spend at that bus stop.

Having lost all bearings, I sat on a bench with my head tucked in between my knees. I felt someone nudge me from the back. My stomach began to churn. When I raised my head, I saw Kheera standing in front of me. I felt relieved and happy. He explained why he was late. He had to make sure he had enough money and while organizing funds, he had missed the bus. Since he had to take another bus, his arrival was delayed. Whatever the matter, I was relieved and at peace. If Bapu had not been so adamant and had consented to our marriage, we would not have had to suffer this plight. Why can't these old people understand us?

We sat close to each other on the bus to Goa. People sitting nearby were staring at us as we drifted off to sleep, every once in a while, with our heads on each other's laps. We were like birds released from a cage. As the bus passed through the hilly roads and the driver applied sudden brakes, we would hold each other in a tight embrace.

Kheera kept spending the money he had on buying things like mirchi bhajji, fruit and other sundry items. We were left with a little change. I also had some small change. If we were not able to find some job immediately, it would be nothing but misery. Kheera knew that a few people from his settlement were working in Vasco. He began to look for them. We were not able to trace any of them. We were a little scared. We wandered around different places and finally reached a slum where some labourers were settled. People from different places were living there. One family took a liking to us. They got us engaged in construction work. Kheera had worked as a mason in and around his settlement. It came in handy now. He began to work with mason Nagappa and picked up the skills very well. Days passed by, and we were earning well. There are several means to earn money in a city. We went to a contractor who was prepared to pay us better wages.

Since Kheera was working as an independent mason, he was earning one hundred rupees a day, while I earned twenty-five rupees. This was three times more than what we would earn at home. By now I had given birth to two children. Nagappa's wife was a great support to me. Though we belonged to two different communities and our ways of living were different, these things did not matter in urban societies. It was possible for us to live together, forgetting the differences in our lifestyles.

I was planning to save some money so that I could send my children to school to educate them and make them wise. Kheera had also behaved in a responsible manner till the children were born. When we had no work, we would go to the beach for a stroll. We would walk together, hand in hand. We would roam about freely like the birds in the sky after eating ice-cream or sipping on soft drinks. I felt very shy looking at the scantily dressed, fair-skinned men and women lying on the beach. However, Kheera took it casually and said we are free here to enjoy ourselves. He would invite me to swim in the sea just like them. I would vehemently oppose the idea.

Once, when we had finished work, Kheera asked me to go back to the hut while he went somewhere else. Though I finished cooking and put the children to bed and sat waiting for him, he did not return. He came back rather late, fully drunk. He was brought to the hut by a companion of his. Kheera began to shout and rant. He was not prepared to eat his food. 'Your father is a scoundrel. He was not prepared to give you in marriage to me. You know why? Because I did not have any money, isn't that so? Look at me now, the way I am earning.' He went on shouting incoherently. I was also upset with father. Unable to tolerate Bapu's obstinacy and wrong decisions, I had decided to elope with this fellow. But when Kheera began to abuse my father, I lost my temper. My father was not a bad person. In fact, he had worked hard and grown old and mature. His ambition was that everyone around him should prosper. He wanted everyone to possess a small piece of land and a house to live in.

When Kheera began to abuse him, my love for my father surged to the surface. He used to dote on me when I sang and danced. He loved me more than he loved Hari and Loku. Mother would get angry with me and scold me for refusing to do some chores. At such times, father would support me and chide her. I was angry with Kheera for being drunk, and his abusing my father enraged me further. I was also worried about the family disintegrating due to such behaviour. I was greatly disturbed. I sought inspiration from the deity Mariyamma. 'You are attempting to slit the throat of the woman who has full faith in you. Don't you understand? If you behave like this, what will be the fate of our children tomorrow? Will you give them empty coconut shells as begging bowls? Who are you to abuse my father?' Raising my voice and shouting at him, I slapped him hard on his face and pushed him to a corner. He became quiet and fell asleep. By morning he was normal. 'I was very tired. As I began to drink, I felt like drinking more and continued to do so. I wanted to get rid of my aching body. Therefore, I began to drink and the result was this. You made my body ache much more last night. Look, my face is bruised. Are you still angry with me?'

'Could I help getting angry with you? Do you think I should have felicitated you?'

'Whatever happened has happened, let us put this behind us, I shall not drink in future, are you happy?'

I somehow kept Kheera under my control. Because I raised a hue and cry that day, he would have an occasional drink but keep it within limits. I did not mind this. I was afraid that if I tried to exercise complete control over him, it would have an adverse effect. We discussed our responsibilities whenever we got an opportunity. My aim was to make him understand his responsibilities.

Ours was a happy marriage. After begetting two children, we felt we were really on cloud nine. It seems the goddess was jealous of our happy life. A building was under construction. The house belonged to a person from our region who had migrated to Vasco and had amassed a lot of wealth. On that fateful day, Kheera had gone to work ahead of me. It was the day when the concrete roof had to be cast. It was because of this he had left home early, in a hurry. By the time I finished cooking, packed lunch and went to the site with the two children, the concrete work was about to be completed.

The lady of the house was supervising the work. Ever since the construction work had begun, I had developed a liking for her. I set the children down, and got ready to begin work. The landlady went in and brought some sweetmeats for my children. She also brought some of her children's used clothes and pushed them into my bundle. It was drizzling. 'It might begin to rain heavily, work fast,' the landlord cautioned the workers. The contractor hastened the workers who were standing around by threatening them. The mixer was churning concrete. It swallowed huge quantities of sand, cement, water and jelly and spewed out the concrete mix. I stood near the mixer and passed on the baskets filled with concrete. The baskets began to ascend to the top floor quickly, racing with each other. Similarly, empty baskets were hurtling down in quick succession. Everyone was working quickly, like machines. All of a sudden, there was a thud – the sound of someone falling down. Repeated questions of 'What happened?' remained unanswered. Everyone gathered around the fallen body. Someone shouted, 'Kheera has lost his balance and fallen down.' My heart missed a beat.

Kheera had fallen down, unconscious. 'Whatever has happened? Mother Mariyamma, Saathbhavani!' Muttering these words to myself, I pushed through the crowd to reach him and placed my hand on his heart. It was beating rapidly and continuously. 'Sevalal, please save his life,' I began to wail, praying fervently. The people gathered around tried to console me, saying, 'Keep quiet, nothing has happened.'

It started raining heavily. It was not possible to stop the work. In spite of this, the landlord got us a vehicle to go to the hospital. Kheera was bodily lifted and placed in the vehicle. Cuddling the children, who were crying, I also got into the vehicle. We huddled together like wet sparrows. After a while, Kheera opened his eyes and uttered a moan. I felt a little reassured then. Kheera was examined thoroughly in the hospital. He could not stand up. The doctor said, 'He has to stay here for about a month. Since he landed on his knees, both the kneecaps are broken. Luckily, his head is not hurt.' The landlady, the landlord and the contractor often visited the hospital to enquire about him. They asked me not to worry about the expenses involved. Great people! May they live long and happily! I am a person born with ill luck. Who can save me from my misfortunes? Kheera recovered. But he was rendered lame and had to support himself on two crutches.

He was deeply disheartened. 'Zimri, I have become lame. I need to survive on your earnings.' He wept bitterly. It became difficult to lead an independent life after the treatment in the hospital was over, during which period the landlord had taken had taken care of us. What more help could they offer? How long can one support us? Kheera used to spend his time sitting in the hut, looking after the children, and I went out to work. But my earnings were not adequate to take care of the entire family; life became difficult. Though the landlord had taken care of the hospital expenses, I had spent all our savings on other sundry expenses. Now we were left with nothing. Kheera occasionally demanded money for a drink. He was feeling bored sitting at home all the time. Once in a while I brought him a drink. Our life limped along in this manner.

Once, when I went towards the bus stand after working the whole day, I found a man looking at me rather intently. I began to wonder why he was staring at me. I thought he looked familiar. 'Whosoever it may be, let me head home,' I thought, and started walking briskly towards home to feed my hungry children and the husband who would be waiting for me, when the man called me by my name, 'Oh, Zimri!' When I went close to him and took a good look at him, I recognized him. It was Damla. Having seen a person from the Thanda after several years I was overcome with both happiness and surprise. He told me that he had come with his entire family and that they were seated in the bus stand. I went along with him and spoke to each one of them. They urgently needed a place to stay. I said they could stay with us for the time being. All of us started walking towards the hut carrying with us all their goods and chattel. Though Kheera felt happy to meet these people, he was not particularly fond of Damla and maintained his reserve. After dinner, Damla gave us all the news of the Thanda. He told us about the sale of the grounds and his decision to move over here with his share of the money. He narrated how they had fought for cultivating it earlier, and the injury suffered by father in the fight. He also mentioned that father was in Vijayapura at present, with Hari, undergoing treatment.

I did not know anything about any of this. I was disturbed to learn that father had lost his mental balance. I also learnt that Kasanu and others had not been in favour of selling the grazing grounds. But with the help of Loku, things had transpired smoothly. Damla tried to console me, 'If Somalya Nayak was around, this transaction might not have happened so easily. He would have been stubborn and tried to stop the sale. Loku is worldly wise. He is now a member of the panchayat. He is an important person. He goes to various places, he has made friends with many important people. His ways of thinking and practical approach to life are lacking in Kasanu and Nayak. Whatever it may be, Nayak should not have suffered like this. He may be getting better now. You don't worry about these things...there are several ways of earning an income in a city. What do we have in our Thanda or the village? Just mud! Here you can engage yourself in one job or the other.' In spite of this, he had felt bad when he left the Thanda with his family and all his belongings.

When they left the place, their dog followed them. However, many times they tried to drive it away by pelting stones at it, it continued to follow them. Whenever it was hit by a stone, it would moan, but continue to follow them. Finally, out of desperation, Damla pulled out a vine and used it as a rope to tie down its legs and leave it behind. As he said this, he became very sad. Damla and his family stayed with us for a few days. Whenever Damla went out, he would bring something to eat for both his children and our children. On some days, he would be completely drunk and keep shouting. He had a lot of money with him now. He did not like the place we lived in. He decided to settle down elsewhere, and one fine day, he left us. Though he thought one could earn a good living in a city, both Kheera and I wondered whether he would earn any money at all.

I was troubled by memories of my mother and father. I was very sad to know my father's condition. Mother used to narrate her life story to me once in a while. When she came into the house as a new bride, she was greatly troubled by her mother-in-law who would unnecessarily complain about her to her son and make him beat her. She was a formidable woman. Husband and wife could not even speak to each other lovingly in her presence. She often used to advise her son that a man should rule over his wife. My mother was a clever woman. She would sell fruits, berries, fodder, faggots, greens and sundry things and bring in more and more money. It was her earnings that helped my parents educate me and my siblings. Father began to understand this gradually. He stopped troubling mother. Her mother-in-law also grew old. It was only then that an understanding began to develop between my mother and my father.

I don't know what state father is in now. I am not sure what problems mother must be enduring. I thought it would be better to return to the Thanda rather than live here alone with a lame husband. I was steeped in memories of my father and mother.

I also learnt that Loku was now a rich man. It is better to go to a place where we have our kith and kin. When I shared these thoughts with Kheera, he agreed with me.

Twenty-two

(Hari is the narrator)

I will tell you what happened after I brought father and mother to Vijayapura. It was not an ordinary task to keep them in my house in Vijayapura for five years. Father's behaviour was rather strange after he received a blow on his head and serving a prison term. He would either sit quietly for hours or talk to himself continuously. It was necessary to consult a neurologist to treat him.

Both my parents were unhappy with my marriage. They had attended the marriage merely as a formality. They could not accept the fact that I announced my marriage all of a sudden. But all this is now an old story. They could not sever the relationship or the bond as parents. How can I forget them? Father was keen on me getting educated and had always encouraged me to focus on my studies. He lived a frugal life to ensure I received a good education. Later, I was awarded some scholarships and after that I was not much of a burden to him. That's another matter.

The first problem that both father and mother encountered after coming here was using the toilets. Early in the morning, father took a pot of water and got ready to go to the fields to relieve himself. The fields were at least two to three kilometres away from my house. I explained to him that such things are not possible here and said, 'Use the toilet here.' He got disturbed and said, 'How can one defecate inside the house?' However, with no other option left, he began to use the toilet inside our house. But he continued to feel embarrassed. He would use the toilet much before any of us woke up. Mother felt uncomfortable as well. 'Che, che, I don't want to do this in the house,' she said. Finally, being helpless, she also started using the in-house toilet. When I shared this terrible problem with my colleagues in the office, they had a hearty laugh.

After a few days, mother said, 'A toilet is not a bad arrangement. In the Thanda, we had to sit behind bushes and if men passed that way, we would feel very uncomfortable.' But father continued to oppose the idea. He expressed his displeasure by saying, 'How can you compare the comfort of walking across to the fields to relieve yourself with this system of defecating inside the house? I don't understand the ways of this world. What a bad practice!' Father was mostly able to participate in a conversation and speak coherently and respond to questions appropriately. But when he was alone, he would go on muttering to himself. He would laugh or cry for no reason. Sometimes, he would look into the distance and shout expletives, 'Scoundrels! Bastards!' Sometimes, he would clap his hands and sing bhajans.

After seeking an appointment with the doctor, I took father to meet him. The doctor said we need to go for a check-up once every fortnight and that it would take some time for the brain to be restored to its normal state. 'Since he needs constant medical supervision, it is better for him to stay with you,' he suggested.

Kamala, my wife, was from an affluent family. Her father had helped me get this job. I thought it was essential for me to keep her informed about my parents. 'Father and mother are old people; it is necessary for us to make some adjustments. Both of them have struggled a lot in life. They should live in comfort with us.' She approved this proposal. 'Why should I have any objection to that? In fact, they will be a source of support to us,' she said. I felt satisfied with her response. 'But there is one thing to be noted,' she continued.

'What?'

'We live in a colony. Many people do not know that we are Lambadas. Therefore, it is not proper for your mother to be dressed as a Lambada woman. Let us immediately buy some saris and blouses for her.' I thought Kamala's suggestion was reasonable. It is necessary for us to gel with the people around us. We should not stick out like a sore thumb. Is it appropriate for mother to appear in her traditional dress when we have visitors? The very next day both of us went to market and bought saris and blouses. I broached the topic with them. 'We need to live in a dignified manner in a civilized society. It is necessary to give up our traditional dress. At least as long as mother stays with us, let her wear saris,' I pleaded. Father became furious with me. 'What will happen if the neighbours get to know we are Lambadas? Is it demeaning for you? Is it not true that we are Lambadas? Are Lambadas inferior? We are a big society, we have a big society. Why do you rant?'

Mother came forward to pacify father and stopped him from going further, 'You keep quiet, I'll deal with the matter.' She turned to me and said, 'Look here Hari, we do not mind how you live. We don't make demands on how your wife should dress and live. But please don't force me to change. Leave me alone and let me be as I wish to be. If you don't like this, please let us know. We shall go back.' Kamala, sensing that the matter going out of control, silenced me by gently pinching me and whispering, 'Let's leave it at that.' I did not want to prolong the matter and further trouble father who had already suffered a mental setback. But Kamala went inside with anger clearly writ on her face.

Once mother started living with us, Kamala dismissed the domestic help who used to wash utensils and keep the house clean. Mother did all the chores with pleasure. Since our house was close to the cement factory, dust from the factory filled the entire house. Occasionally, the density of dust was heavy enough to choke people, making it difficult for them to breathe. In spite of that, the house always looked clean and presentable because mother used to sweep the floor often and wipe the dust off the furniture. In the afternoons, she would clean the grains and cereals to keep them in separate bundles. After her arrival, my wife had ample rest and I was also more comfortable.

It became necessary to impose certain restrictions on father who always remained moody. I was afraid he would be run over by a bus or a car if he went out. It is a very difficult task to cross roads in a city. Therefore, I asked him not to leave the house. He felt bored sitting idle at home. 'What do I do sitting like this in the house?' he began to whimper. Then I relented and said, 'When you feel bored, go and sit in the park in front of the house.' It was not much of a park. There were barely two trees. There was a platform under those trees. Nearby was a garbage bin where after their meal everyone deposited the plates made by stitched leaves. Dogs and pigs would fight with each other over these leaves for the leftover food in them. Some garbage pickers also planned to get to the leftover food in those leaves before the dogs and pigs had their share.

Father could not sit idly in the park. When I saw him pick up each piece of garbage and deposit it in the bin, I got angry and told him sternly, 'You should not do such work. That is the job of the municipality. We have a status. Our prestige will be damaged if you do such things.'

'What is wrong with that? It is an open place in front of our house. I go and sit there, I clean the place where I want to sit, that's all,' he said.

'I want you to be comfortable, therefore I need to tell you all this. Besides, you have to go often to the doctor for consultation. How can you be doing such things?' Since then, he stopped going out of the house, but would lie down in a corner all day, wrapping himself completely in sheets. There was no interaction with anybody. My mother tried to convince me to let him go out.

'He will feel bored. If he goes out and sits there, he will feel a little relaxed. Give him that concession.' I felt she was right and relented. He was once again cheerful. But he began to spend most of his time out there. When monsoon set in, he picked up a pick-axe and shovel and began to make pits on the ground of the park. He filled the pits with soil and the garbage that was lying around. Bowing to his demands, I bought him a few saplings. He spent most of his time planting them and tending them.

As he sat in the park and observed the boys and girls going to school and college, father must have wished that the children in the Thanda had similar opportunities. 'I don't know what the state of affairs of the school in the Thanda is. We had a good teacher in the Thanda. I don't know what happened after all the trouble erupted. Why don't you get a few of the children in the Thanda who are good at studies and keep them with you? Let them stay in the room in the backyard and they can go to a school here. Rupli will cook food for them. Let a few children receive a good education like you and make progress.'

In a way, what he said was reasonable. But of late, my wife had been insisting on our buying a television, which had made its appearance all over the town. She also felt that if we had a refrigerator, food will keep longer. I need to buy these things. Our needs were growing. Therefore, I told him rather sternly, 'You don't understand. The salary we earn is hardly sufficient in a city. Should I run a boarding home here?' Father began muttering to himself angrily at my rebuke and went to the park to tend to the plants.

When I got annoyed and said that his work in the park was crossing limits, he once again withdrew and sat inside the house all day. As he sat like this, he would recall his past life in the Thanda – the way his mother would dispense justice, the community living in the Thanda and other things. 'I had lofty dreams; "let my Thanda be evergreen, let it be the home for toil and hard work, let our people be farmers and sow seeds to grow greenery." All this has now been rendered futile. A costly slip was induced between the cup and the lip, those rascals! Did we aspire for their share? What injustice did we do to them? We were very happy and felt that we had the moon and stars in our hands when the grazing grounds stood verdant with full grown crops!' Knowing that it was not good for his health to get emotionally excited in this manner, I had to tell him rather firmly, 'Father, what is the use in thinking of the past? Whatever had to happen has happened. Just forget everything and stay calm.' But he continued, 'Write a letter to Loku. Find out what has happened to the grazing grounds. Find out how he is doing.' He seemed concerned. 'Don't worry about unnecessary things,' I told him, 'I will write a letter to him asking him to come here at his convenience.' Comforting father in this manner had become routine.

If father spent most of his mornings sitting in the park, Kamala would spend the whole day sitting or sleeping in her room. Left alone, mother felt bored and went to the neighbours for a chat. Kamala complained about this as soon as I got back home from work one evening. 'Why should she go to other people's houses? Each one is engaged in various chores of their own. Or they may be resting. They will pass snide remarks afterwards. This is not the Thanda where you go and visit anyone at any time. Give some proper advice to your mother.' I thought it was my fate to get caught between Kamala on the one side and my mother on the other. After a while, I broached the topic with mother in a relaxed manner. 'The world of the Thanda is different from the world of this town. We need to live according to the norms of this place. It is not proper to go visiting others.'

'What life is this? Living like owls! Everyone keeps the doors shut. Nobody talks to others, there is no sharing of happiness and sorrows. The other day, when the old woman in the next house died, there was no weeping or moaning, there was no sound of any kind, no one knew when she died, and when the body was taken away for the last rites. If this had happened in the Thanda, the whole Thanda would have come together.'

Once, we ran out of vegetables and Kamala asked father to go to a nearby shop and buy some. Once he left home, mother felt a little uncomfortable about him going alone and followed him. As they were buying vegetables, I believe two or three bulls ran into the vegetable shop, upset the baskets and also hit a couple with a child who were riding a scooter, bringing them to the ground. When I got back home in the evening, mother narrated the entire incident to me and said that had she not been there, father would have come back with fractured hands or legs. I said, 'There are quite a few stray bulls hovering around the town. They attack people for no reason and destroy anything that falls in their path. If they are stopped, they knock us down to the ground and pierce us with their horns. Nobody can do anything. We need to be as careful as possible,' I cautioned them.

Presently, Kamala became pregnant and was sent to her parent's house for confinement. The responsibility of managing the entire house fell on mother. When she sat by me and served me food with all her affection, I remembered my younger days when she used to feed me. If I went for my bath, she would follow me to massage my back. When I expressed annoyance, saying, 'I will be late for office, you move away from here,' she would still apply soap on my back before leaving. The freedom she could not enjoy when my wife was around, she savoured now and moved around as she pleased. Occasionally, she used to croon her old songs. Either because of the cold climate here, or because of the excessive dust from the cement factory, mother began to cough and developed some phlegm in her lungs. She did not want to go to a doctor. Instead she made a decoction of dry ginger and some herbs and drank it. Perhaps it would have subsided in due course of time. But eager for her to be completely cured of the cough before my wife arrived with the child, I took her to a doctor. When I told the doctor, 'She has been wheezing and coughing very badly and needs to be cured quickly,' he prescribed some tiny tablets. The next day, dramatically, there was no cough. 'The tablets are very effective,' she said. She took the tablets every day. After a few days, however, she began to cough even more severely than earlier. She kept an aluminum vessel by her side to spit out the phlegm. A friend of mine visited us and took a look at the tablets given to mother. 'Why are you giving her these? True, the cough will subside immediately after consuming these, but subsequently, the consequences will be dangerous. These are steroids, life-saving drugs, to be administered only in an emergency.' I took her to another doctor and had her examined once again. Mother's cough became more intense. Either because of my haste or the wrong prescription, mother became an asthma patient.

Kamala came back with a baby boy. Mother was very happy to see her grandson. But seeing her cough, Kamala called me aside and said, 'Your mother should not come near the child. It is better that the two of them move into the outhouse.' I was wondering how to break this news to mother and finally decided to use some scientific reasons. My mother consented, saying, 'That's fine, what is wrong with it? The child should be all right, that's all.' But father seemed upset. I felt very uneasy as well, having to ask them to move into the outhouse, which in this case was a room at the back of the house. What could I do? If father had been his former self, he would perhaps never have tolerated this. He must have kept quiet only because he was in a peculiar state now. He did not speak to me for a few days. Perhaps mother pacified him later.

Mother could not live without seeing her grandson. Whenever she felt all right, she came out of the outhouse and took a good look at the child. When she saw Kamala feeding the child milk from a bottle, she intervened, saying, 'That is not the way, you should breastfeed the child.' Kamala curtly shot back, 'I know what I am doing.' When mother tried to give her some homemade nutritives, she refused them, saying, 'I have no need for them. The doctor has given me medicines and tonic.' I thought of sending my parents back to the Thanda as it occurred to me that they were being mentally tortured in the city.

I wrote a letter to Loku asking him to come at once. When he came and narrated details of the cultivation in the grazing grounds, father felt very happy. He also informed him about the efforts that were in progress to have the lands registered. 'We will come with you,' said father, expressing his anxiety to return, but Loku decided not to take them back. 'You may come after the registration deeds are ready. In the meantime, let mother get cured of her asthma,' was his honey-laced response.

Loku used to keep me updated about the events transpiring in the Thanda. I told father and mother only that which I thought would not upset them. I did not inform them about the unfavourable decision given by the government with respect to the grazing grounds. I informed them about the court's verdict and Loku's efforts in having the lands registered in our names. I did not divulge the news of people selling their lands to Mr Desai for money. Under such circumstances, if father went back to the Thanda, he would be further upset, which could affect his health badly, I reasoned. Therefore, I tried to stall his return to the Thanda. Though this was my strong wish, an incident took place that went against all my intentions.

Whenever somebody visited us, whether they were friends or guests, father would come and sit with us. He had a great desire to talk to someone. When my bank manager visited us, he came and sat along with us. I introduced my father to the manager. He greeted him with a lot of respect. Tea and snacks were served. The manager was fairly familiar with our customs and culture. He did not miss any opportunity to praise our people for their industriousness. He spoke to father with much affection. 'I have heard about Sevalal. Did a person like him really exist? His having gone to the heaven with the goddess, having an argument with her there...can one really believe all this?'

'He did exist, and he still exists. It is also true that he argued and won.'

'No, it might have been a legend.'

'What does that mean?'

'Means, he must have been a fictitious character; it must be a story from the puranas. He might not have existed, and even if he did, such events might not have taken place.'

'He exists. He is part of my system, he flows through my veins, he responds to my call and shows his presence. Do you understand? It is a clever talk, but don't talk nonsense.' When father uttered the last words his eyes were burning red, there was a stammer in his speech. 'Oh, please, leave it at that,' said the manager, and got up to leave. I went out to see him off and said in a low whisper, 'Please don't misunderstand. He speaks like this as he is not mentally stable.'

'That is all right,' said the manager and left my place.

I went back in and raised my voice against father. This was the first time I had used such a tone with him. 'In the first place it is wrong on your part to come and sit with us when we have friends and guests. Once you sit, you need to be polite and decent in your manner. He is my boss. You don't understand what to say and what not to say to him. How can you speak to him, my boss, so rudely?'

'I don't care who he is. Why did he say such things about Sevalal? He talks as if he knows a lot. He is a man with just a brain. What a great man Sevalal is! He is settled in our bosom. How can these people understand the inner voice?'

'That is his opinion. Why should you get angry?'

'Your boss is important to you. You do not have any love for the way you were brought up or the place where you were born, you don't have any attachment or a sense of pride.'

I was very disturbed with father's behaviour that day. Though I kept quiet, he did not eat anything the whole day and shut himself in the outhouse, shouting continuously. My mother tried to pacify him.

It was perhaps midnight. I was feeling drowsy. I heard someone singing and was woken up immediately. I heard prayers to Sevalal being sung.

> *satyaguru satyaguru sevalal baapu*
> *thona namaskar*
> *bavan barode vaalo dhole ghode vaalo*
> *soneri kalase eelo*
> *akhanda brahmachari bharose baari*
> *sevalal malkeri thapasseri*
> *uudo taalaa samakar chithoram pathokar*
> *aasa vaaleri aasa purikar*
> *baapu thone namaskar*

Father Sevalal, veritable lord of truth;
My salutations to you.
Shower the blessing of prosperity
As you ride along on a white horse

Eternal Celibate, you fill everyone with confidence
When they sight you with your golden crown

. . . .

. . . .

Father, my salutations to you

When father begun to pray to Sevalal in the form of bhajans, Kamala lost her patience. 'What is this? What behaviour is this? What will the neighbours think of us? What does it mean to sing these Lambada songs in the middle of the night? Your father has sold our reputation cheaply. He has gone mad. How could he insult your boss in the evening? I am tired of them living with us. I have tolerated it far too long. I thought my mother-in-law would be a support to me in my housework. But let us employ someone from outside if need be. It is me or them for you now. Will you go and ask him to seal his lips, or shall I get up and go myself?' I kept sitting there helplessly, without a word.

> *bhandar khan bharpurkar*
> *thaar namero laago bhog*
> *lokor upar saayi vejo*
> *lal thona namaskar*

> We offer a feast in your name,
> For you have filled our granaries to the full;
> Have mercy on your folk
> My salutations to you

Kamala opened the door and angrily marched to the outhouse and knocked on the door. 'Will you shut up or not? What do you have against us, come out with it. If you want to humiliate us in public, continue to sing like this. I am terribly tired because of you. You have been behaving like our enemies!' When my father heard her ranting in this manner, he became quiet. Though Kamala went back into the house, I continued to pace up and down outside. There appeared to be a minor tiff in progress between mother and father. 'I can forgive the daughter-in-law. But even he, the son, does not understand me,' said father, heaving a deep sigh. After I went back in, Kamala wanted to sleep close to me. I pushed her away and slept at a distance. Yes, father is someone I have not been able to understand fully! How does it matter to her? I felt a severe pang of guilt. Somalya Nayak, the chief of a thanda, a person who had earned a lot of respect from his people, is now living in a pitiable state in his son's house! The son who he has educated with hope and affection has been behaving like this. Why is father speaking in a strange way these days? What is it that I can do?

When I got back home from work in the evening the next day, mother and father were not there. When I asked Kamala, she feigned ignorance. When I enquired with the old woman selling groundnuts near the park, she said both of them had left in the afternoon with their bags. I looked for them everywhere. I went and searched around the bus stand and returned home without being able to find them.

Twenty-three

(Kasanu is the narrator)

Around dusk, I was sitting on the terrace, filling sacks with grain. The worm-infested grain had been spread on the terrace to be dried in the sun. The worms were not dead. I was worried about a drizzle in the night, so I was filling them in sacks. The worms had drilled through the solid jowar grains and made them hollow. Man, who is around five to six feet, is also burrowing through the earth like these worms.

The sun had begun to set, lending the earth a reddish hue, the hue of turmeric mixed with lime or that of blood. As I gazed into the distance, I could see two people walking straight towards the Thanda. Often, they would bend down to examine this or that along the road. Who could they be? I raised my head, and out of curiosity my gaze began to follow them. She was certainly one of us, the Lambadas. She had tucked a bundle on her side. The man had a bag in his hand. He was in a coat and had a turban on his head. He was wearing a dhoti that just about crossed his kneecap. Who could these people be? They seemed to be making enquiries and were headed towards my house. Goodness! Somalya and his wife Rupli! Five years ago, I had persuaded Hari to take them away to Vijayapura. They could live there happily, forgetting the troubles that enveloped this place. They had to go past my house to reach their house.

I climbed down from the terrace quickly. 'How are you, Kasanu?' said Somalya as he approached me. 'Aav, aav,' I invited them both inside and called out to Lali, 'Look who is here!' Lali came out and exclaimed, 'Oh! Rupli! It's been so long since I last saw you! Uncle, please do come in!' She went in and brought water in a pot to help them wash their hands, feet and face and refresh themselves. I took the bag from Somalya's hand and asked him to wash his face. He placed his turban on the platform, washed his face and came in and sat on the porch with a sigh. Rupli went inside with Lali.

'What is this? The Thanda is difficult to recognize. It does not look like our Thanda. It has changed so much! What has happened to this Thanda? How many buildings! Such heavy traffic! I had to make enquiries as if I had come into a strange town. Besides, my eyesight is getting worse.'

'Oh, that's a long story. Have some rest first, and I will let you know everything in detail.'

'Let us go to our house. I wonder if Loku is around.'

'No, Loku now lives in a huge house resembling a palace. His house is near the quarry. What can you do there now, in this darkness? Don't go to your old house. Don't go to Loku's house. Stay with us for the night. You may go home in the morning and clean the house.'

Somalya asked several questions, 'Why does Loku not stay here? Does he not like the Thanda?'

'Never mind that, how is Hari? I hope both of you were comfortable in Vijayapura, forgetting all of us. How is it that you have come away all of a sudden?'

'Why should we talk about all those things now? Why did you not inform me about Ramji uncle's passing away?'

'He was old. Besides, I knew both of you were not keeping well. Therefore, I decided to keep quiet.'

'He was an elderly person to all of us. He was one who knew our history. He knew our customs, culture, and ways of living, our ancestry, stories and legends.'

In the meantime, Lali brought us tea in tumblers. Dhenya, my son, arrived home, tethered the bullocks to the post and hung the bridle and the whip on the hook. Noticing Somalya, he said, 'When did you come, uncle?' He went out after formal greetings and exchanges. After dinner, we carried our bedding up to the terrace as the clouds had cleared. We did not forget to take the choota. 'Hari has made me give up the habit of smoking choota. But light it now, I shall have a couple of puffs and give it back to you. It has been long time since I have smoked,' said Somalya. Having taken his two or three puffs, he began to ask me questions about the Thanda. I did not know where to begin. I wanted to share with him everything that had hurt me.

'It has not remained the Thanda of my dreams. I have never thought of Loku as an outsider. He is like my son. It is not necessary for me to tell you how the two of us have grown together. But how can I not divulge the sorrow that is troubling me. Loku has not taken after you. He is made of different mettle. Why did he become like this? He is mainly responsible for all these changes that have taken place in the Thanda. He received good support from that Thukya. He became a member of the panchayat and began to frequent Kalluru. His growth began from that point of time. To begin with, he got us all together and with the help of Hiralal, he put in a lot of effort in acquiring the grazing grounds. Though the government reversed all our efforts and stopped us from getting the grazing grounds, we went to court and got a decision in our favour. But I do not know what promises were made by Mr Desai in confidence. Loku changed his stand overnight. He rolled out a red carpet for commissioning quarries. If he had not played a leading role in facilitating this, perhaps we would still have the grazing grounds with us. All the dreams that we had dreamt together were washed away. Where are those grazing grounds? The grazing grounds that were so dear to us! The grazing grounds of our dreams have been shattered to pieces. Even Hiralal, who we trusted, cheated us. We were left without any support. Our desire to obtain a small piece of land and cultivate it together and remain as one community has been reduced to ashes. You may brand me a stubborn fellow. With the money I received, I bought a small piece of land near Kalluru. It is not as fertile as the grazing grounds. What could I do? The young calf I had had grown into a bull. I have bought one more bullock. My son has been engaged in agriculture. But most people took the money and squandered it. The sight of wads of currency, which they had never seen earlier, made our people lose their mind. They are going back to square one.

'I had placed a lot of hope in Loku. I had never thought he would go astray in this manner. I appealed to him fervently, "The money Mr Desai will give will not last long with our people. Let's not go for this. Let's retain the grazing grounds." It was like a dog barking against the hills, a dog that gets overrun and killed by a bull. Loku was intoxicated with money. Many of our huts have been replaced by Janata houses. Both Loku and the panchayat president made lots of money while allotting each house. I also understand he acquired a share of the money for facilitating the sale of the grazing grounds to Mr Desai. He was possessed with a desire to turn into a rich man overnight. And he believed that the path he was following was the right one. Today, tractors, motorcycles and trucks roam around the Thanda the whole day roaring and making a deafening noise. Merchants dealing in stone have come and settled in Kalluru and are carrying on their business. Today, our Thanda has come to be well known because of the granite. People are coming here from different parts of the country and the world to buy stones. Every day we have been a witness to this looting.

'Limber jhadera het besan nasaab karetho – You used to sit on the platform under the neem tree and advise people. Your mother also sat there and dispensed justice. We would all sit there in the evening and relax. That neem tree had given many of us peace and comfort! If you asked someone to swear by holding a branch of the tree, a person who had lied would begin to shiver. Where is that sacred tree now? They said the road had to be widened to accommodate electric poles. They decided that it was imperative to cut the tree and uproot it completely. Sevalal's temple, which was beside it, was also removed. All my appeals to Loku and his cohorts to save the tree and the temple fell on deaf ears. Loku argued, "What is there in this temple? There is a boulder at the back, acting as a wall, and a roof of sorts overhead. Inside, there are two round stones. We will build a first class cement temple, just wait and see." I said, "Yes, you may build a temple. You may also plant a new tree. But in this original temple and the tree lies our lives, our souls, our identity. Your father, his mother and several elders have come under this tree to advise and dispense justice. This neem tree is a divine persona for us. It has protected us from disease and illnesses; it has warded off our boredom and healed our children of their bodily sores; verily, it has been a panacea for us. The entire Thanda would be filled with the fragrance of its flowers and tender shoots around the time of

Ugadi, the New Year. We have developed a bond with this tree and the platform. Bonds do not develop just between two people. We have nourished our dreams under this tree which has with its deep roots sucked sustenance from the earth and stood tall and wide. We have thought deeply. We have shared our happiness and sorrows. You have played under its shade as young boys. Your sisters have danced here. Our women folk have sung songs under it. All this will become memories of the past." Do you know what Loku's response to this was? "You and father both belong to the old generation. You don't understand anything. You want to progress, yet you want to retain all this. How can that be possible? The time when we travelled in a cart harnessed to bullocks is long gone. It is the time of cars and airplanes. If we want to progress, these changes are inevitable. If we only talk of morals and sentiments, we will have to remain where we are." The tree was like a pinnacle to the whole of Thanda. When it was felled, none of these boys felt hurt. That place appears so desolate now. You will see it for yourself tomorrow when you take a stroll. Go towards the hillocks and the lake. The whole hillock has been reduced to smithereens. The place is filled with small stones and fine dust.'

Somalya was stunned. He said, 'Kasanu, that's enough. Don't tell me anything more. I came here to see the greenery of the grazing grounds. I did not know about any of this. Nobody told me. Why should I live any further, Kasanu? Aacho venu – does not mean development in this manner. Where are the people who can empathize with us? The son who lives in the city has his own ways. And this son seems to be on a path to destroy the entire Thanda. Sevalal, why have you brought this upon us? Give sense to these people.'

I cut short my narrative realizing that Somalya was getting distressed. I felt I need not have elaborated all this to him. But I could not help pouring out my sorrow to him. I seemed to have waited all these days to vent. All the emotions that I was filled with seemed to have overflowed uninterruptedly as soon as I saw him. Though I said, 'Okay, have a good sleep, it is already quite late,' he was tossing and turning through the night, his mind clouded with disturbing thoughts. I couldn't get any sleep either. Early in the morning, I must have slipped into slumber. For some reason I woke up with a start. Somalya had gathered himself in a corner and was smoking a choota.

I cursed myself for having narrated all these incidents and disturbing him. But what if I had not told him? He would certainly have come to know about all this later. Was there someone else I could share my thoughts with other than him? He had understood me, and I had understood him well enough. 'Have you had some good sleep?' I asked. 'Yes,' he replied and fell silent. We climbed down from the terrace. Lali had cleaned the porch and was drawing rangoli. He stood there, watching her. He said, 'It has been a long time since I have seen such rangoli.' I wanted to ask, 'Why, was it not drawn in your son's house?' But not wanting to probe further, I kept quiet. After having tea, Somalya and Rupli got ready to go to their house. I asked my son Dhenya to take the key Loku had given us and go with them. He opened the lock and dusted and cleaned the house before coming back home.

Somalya sat at home as if he was in a daze. Rupli tried to persuade him to go out. 'Why are you sitting here like a possessed one? Why don't you go out and take a stroll?' He went out with slow steps and strayed towards the place where the neem tree had stood. Seeing an electric pole in its place, he was overcome with sorrow. The old temples of Mariyamma and Sevalal had vanished without a trace. A few tractors had been parked here and there. Trucks were plying between the hillock and the Thanda. There were houses built for the workers working in the quarry. None of those people recognized him. He began to feel he was in a strange place. When he strolled towards the school, he found that it was

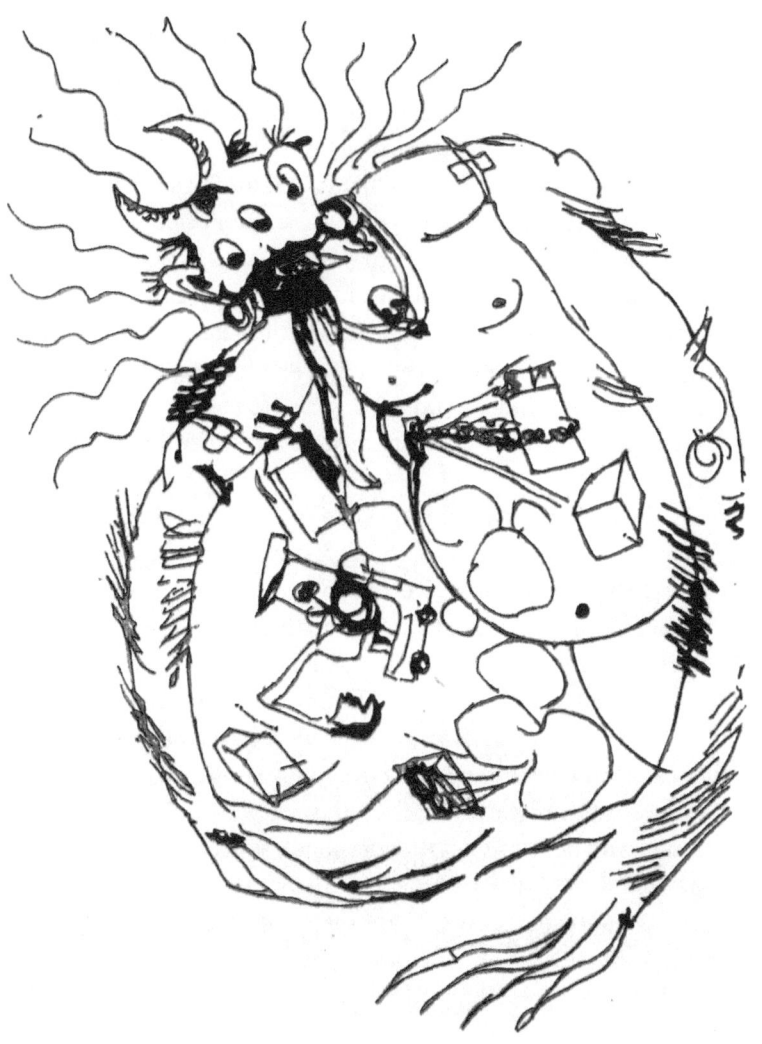

now a larger building. There were two teachers. When he peeped in, he was asked, 'What do you want? Who are you?'

'There is nobody even to recognize me!' The thought saddened him. He slowly walked back home and told Rupli, 'We don't have a place here either. The village has morphed into a town; there are houses, there is electricity. But unlike what we had thought, there is no place for us here. The tree has been uprooted, it has been destroyed without a trace!'

'Why do you talk like a mad man? Whatever has happened to you? Let us learn to adjust to new ways,' Rupli said.

Around afternoon, I went to their house. Somalya was sitting alone, silently. As soon as I went in, Rupli began to complain about her husband, 'If he speaks, he just keeps talking about depressing things; otherwise, he just sits by himself in complete silence. I don't understand what to do. My asthma never seems to get better...whatever we are destined to suffer, let us take it in our stride.'

'What will the two of you do here? Loku stays alone in a big house. If you go and stay there, he may also mend his ways. Therefore, it is better for you to go and stay there,' I suggested. Initially, Somalya did not agree to go there. But he eventually got up and got ready to visit his son, yielding to the pressure. Rupli also got ready and I took them along with me to their son's house.

The road to his house was well laid. It was a road that was laid for cars and trucks to ply on. Beyond his house, on the other side of the road, was the quarry. As we were walking, we saw trucks loaded with heavy stones moving about, squeaking and groaning, spewing dust. A truck loaded with stones was stranded on one side of the road. A few well-dressed stones, cut into cubes, had been scattered around here and there. Somalya was upset at the sight, as he walked along.

As we went further ahead, he asked, 'Where is the lake?' Heaps of dust from the stones was lying there, destroying the last traces of the lake. A crane was loading a huge stone on to a truck. Somalya said, 'Kasanu, I feel like my entrails are being dragged out.' When we peeped into Loku's office, the watchman told us, 'The boss has gone home.' We moved towards the house. I opened the compound gate, went in and knocked on the door, but it never opened. I took the initiative and banged on the door loudly and continuously. An authoritative voice from inside was heard, 'Who's there?'

'It's us! Open the door,' I shouted. Loku came swaying and swaggering opened the door with a bottle in his hand.

When he saw his parents he felt embarrassed, even in that state. He did not ask us to come into the house. We entered the house. A woman who too was drunk was lying on his bed. He quickly closed the door of that room when he saw us noticing her and took us to a different part of the house. 'This is enough. Come let us go away,' Somalya said to Rupli. Rupli grabbed Loku, and scolded him in a loud voice and began to cry. He interrupted, 'Why are you crying? What has happened? I have earned a lot of money. Live here in comfort. Your elder son could not earn much in spite of his education. I have earned a lot. He has informed me about everything on phone. I believe you troubled him when you were there. He seems to have had enough of it because of you. And you should not repeat the same things here. You should not object to anything I do. I know what is right and what is not. Father, you had dreamt of developing the Thanda, I have developed it a hundred fold more than what you had hoped for in these three-four years. Now the Thanda has electricity, taps in houses, a large school and a larger temple; it has grown beyond recognition.' Loku continued to rant in his drunken state. 'I know everything about how you have earned the money and what you have done. You have denuded the hills and hillocks, blocked the lake and its canals, rendered the fertile lands infertile and you boast of having developed the Thanda. I also dreamt of development, but not in your way. Your desire to turn rich overnight has destroyed you! Rupli, if you want to stay back, you may do so, I cannot stay here.' So saying, Somalya began to walk out. 'Both of you should live here. Where else do you want to go? This is also your son's house,' said Loku. But though he tried to persuade his parents to stay, both of them walked out immediately. The entire episode had hurt Somalya deeply.

❖

Somalya's daughter and son-in-law Kheera came to the Thanda. Both Somalya and Rupli felt happy on the arrival of their daughter and son-in-law with their children. But both were saddened for her life was in shambles. Somalya felt a bit comforted at the thought that his daughter and son-in-law's return may mean that they have forgotten everything that had happened and were no longer angry with him. He had nursed a strong feeling of having wronged them. 'You are not angry with me, are you?' he asked her. He poured out his anguish to his daughter. 'I looked for a rich groom to save you from the wrath of poverty. I did not understand your love for each other. Now I realize. I have understood the consequences of recklessly going after this bad money. I realized it soon enough. There is no point growing like a wild buffalo, giving up all your love and affection, throwing to winds morals and character and forgetting human values. That is not necessary, Zimri.'

'Forget it, father. We have put all that behind us. Why are you thinking about all that and worrying yourself? Mother told me that you are very worried about several things of the past. Relax and be at ease.'

'How can I relax, my child, looking at the ravages suffered in life by my dear daughter?'

Rupli, observing her husband's anguish, intervened and said rather angrily and authoritatively, 'Will you keep quiet or not?' He stopped speaking. Rupli turned to Zimri and said, 'Settle down in this Thanda. Your father has always loved you a lot. If you stay here for a while, perhaps he will feel a little better.' When the children began wandering around the place, calling

them 'grandma' and 'grandpa', Somalya felt a little better.

He was perhaps all right for about a month. After that, he once again began talking and muttering to himself while seated in isolation. I used to visit him occasionally and force him to come out for a walk. When he came out, he would again remember the tree and the temple and get disturbed and begin to talk to himself, forgetting my presence.

Duglibai had diabetes. Limbya, her son-in-law, had taken her to Kalluru and later to Nagarkote to consult the doctors. She had no other relatives to depend on. She only had her daughter, Rukki. As son-in-law, Limbya thought this was the least he could do. He spent a considerable amount of money on her treatment. Duglibai was not left with the strength she had earlier. The once strong Duglibai had withered. Both Somalya and I had reposed confidence in Limbya. He had conducted himself well and not belied our faith in him. Panchayat elections were announced. There was one seat shared between the residents of the pariah colony in Kalluru and the Thanda. Loku was contesting once again. He had the power of money. Dhulya, Khubya, myself and a few others thought of nominating Limbya. We thought we need a spirited youngster like Limbya who would work with enthusiasm and sincerity. Besides, we wanted to teach Loku a lesson. We wanted to isolate him so that he would mend his ways. Dhulya, Khubya, his children and I went from house to house canvassing for Limbya. We also went round the pariah colony of Kalluru. We received support from people in every place we went to. Everyone said Loku needs to be taught a lesson. Nobody from the pariah colony was contesting.

'Let two people not contest from the Thanda, let it be just one. Let there be unity,' said Thukya, who came along with a few of his companions and persuaded one of the contestants to withdraw.

'Right, but who should withdraw?' was the question everyone asked.

'Our Thanda has been on the path of progress because of Loku. A lot of development has happened because of him. What do we achieve from making innocent Limbya contest? Let Limbya withdraw,' he said.

It was certain for us that Loku had no clear support. Our intention was to have someone elected who was a selfless worker, who was concerned about our Thanda, who understood our problems and empathized with us. We were sure of winning. But we do not know what miracle happened! When the votes were counted, most of them were in favour of Loku. Once again, Loku was elected. He is believed to have distributed packets of liquor to all the pariah colony dwellers the night before the elections. He had met the leaders there and given them wads of currency and made all the necessary arrangements. The labourers at the quarry who were residents of the Thanda also seemed to have voted in his favour. Loku had made a promise to the youth of the Thanda. 'Some people call our Thanda "Kalluru Thanda" and some others call it "Havan Thanda". We will remove both these names and declare this an independent village. I will call this Lakshmipura and assure you that this will be a revenue division.' All the youngsters clapped for him and welcomed his suggestion. People had voted for him despite knowing the games and tricks he played. We felt very sad. Limbya had also got handbills printed and distributed them. He had also displayed some boards advertising his promises. He had spent money on his campaign.

Dhulya and Khubya wanted to buy a piece of land with the money they had got from Mr Desai, but no piece of good land was available. Therefore, they had taken a small quarry on contract and started their business. All of them had supported and encouraged Limbya in the elections. They had excavated stones and kept them ready to be transported in trucks. But somebody had transported all these stones in the middle of the night without their knowledge. This made them incur a huge loss. Loku had taken money from Khubya with the promise of a police job for his son Dooda. He said that he had handed over the money to the senior official and that the job was guaranteed. But he had not been appointed to the job yet. When he was asked to give back the money, Loku evaded the issue saying he would return the money once the officer gave it back to him.

A few finance companies raised their heads in Kalluru. They announced that they would double the customer's money in a year's time. Loku encouraged our people to invest money in these finance companies. There must have been some understanding between him and these companies. Believing in him, many of our people invested their savings in these companies. The financiers disappeared from the scene with all the money the poor people had saved. Some others lost their money in gambling dens, playing cards or simply by drinking in bars. In a year or so, these people are sure to exhaust all their money and surrender to poverty.

It had been three or four months since Damla had gone to Goa with his wife and children. As he had the money he had got from Mr Desai, he began to spend it lavishly. His wife and children would go to work. He would work for a day and not go to work for the next three days. He also got into gambling. Once, he won a huge sum of money while gambling, and when he was returning home with all the booty a few people attacked him, killed him and escaped with all the money. His wife came back to the Thanda with her children, realizing there was not much she could do in a place where she did not belong. We were all moved to sorrow to know the state of his family and the ill fate he has met in an alien place. His wife narrated the woeful tale after her return to the Thanda.

Recently, one of the labourers from another village engaged in breaking stones fell down and died. The owners of the company paid monetary compensation to his wife and children and silenced them. They paid some more money so that none of the relatives and friends would inform the police. They took care to see that the news did not spread. Hearing of such deaths had become an everyday matter.

The number of festivals in the Thanda has reduced considerably these days. Dancing, singing and community dinners have all been forgotten. Holi is the only festival that still holds sway. But even this festival has undergone rapid changes. It was our custom to take permission from the chief of the Thanda a fortnight in advance to celebrate the festival. Once the permission was given, preparation for the festival would begin. Now people had begun to prepare for the festival without taking any permission from Somalya Nayak. I remembered the folk songs I used to sing in those days.

sole haathero taaro phaag ro ye gujarani
nave haathero, voro dor!
ghumatho av taaro dor ghaghariyo gujarani!
lalakath av taaro dor!
sole takdeeri taari kaanchliya gujarani!
chalkathi av taarakaachi!

Oh, damsel your skirt of sixteen yards
Has a nine yard lace,
Your skirt comes with grandeur and grace
Look, the border it follows,
Damsel, your blouse is made of sixteen coloured pieces
It is brightened by mirrors stuck on it.

Earlier, we used to celebrate all the festivals without any exception in a grand manner. We had to pick up two young people who were ready to get married. The two belonged to different communities. We used to call them 'geriya'. Then, preparations for the Kamanna bonfire were made under the leadership of these young people, but nowadays the boys perform all these rituals as they like. They were practising kolata, the folk dance, but neither the song nor the dance was according to our customs. They were dancing to the tune of a Hindi film song wearing dark glasses with kerchiefs tied round their necks. There was neither melody nor rhythm. As they danced, they were shouting, 'Yaahoo, yaahoo!' There was neither grace nor delicateness. They were jumping around like donkeys. I thought of taking Somalya to the place where they were dancing. I abandoned the idea thinking that it would further depress him. This elderly man was not respected and honoured as he had been in the past. In these last three-four years, several changes had taken place in the Thanda. This soul had cherished dreams about the growth of the Thanda. He had planned several things. I felt very bad that such a person had lost all his prominence.

Realizing that the demand for liquor was quite high during the festival season, our people began preparations to brew liquor. Packets and bottles of liquor sold by the excise department also began to arrive. A shop was opened exclusively for selling this liquor. Besides, the liquor brewed in the Thanda had customers from both within and outside the Thanda. Those who had tried other business and suffered losses as well as those who had spent money recklessly began to brew liquor. Duglibai thought of brewing some liquor so that she could earn some money and fill the coffers that were emptied because of her treatment. She asked her son-in-law to go and buy a few things necessary for the purpose. Limbya had no other choice but to agree with her and reluctantly went to the market. Limbya and Rukki would bury the pots she readied with liquor in pits near the hills in the middle of the night.

Limbya had gone to Nagarkote to buy jaggery. My son Dhenya and I had gone to the fields. It was evening and there were not many people in the Thanda. Rangaraju, the son-in-law of the excise contractor, thought his business would suffer and complained to the police about the illicit distillation, asking them to raid the place. The police came in a van and arrested Damla's wife, Duglibai and a few others and took them away. Rangaraju, who had followed them in his car, went to Limbya's house and asked Rukki, who was breastfeeding her child to get into his car. She asked, 'Why should I get in?' She had recognized him. It was he who had been after her when all of us had gone to Nagarkote earlier. Her heart began to beat fast. 'I have come to know that you have buried pots in different places in the hills. You show them to me. I shall break all the pots and go away. Otherwise, I will have to ask the police jeep to come here again. After breaking the pots, I shall bring you back here and leave you behind, isn't that all right with you?'

'I have a small child. Leave me alone. Being helpless, we are into this business. Have some mercy.'

'I can't leave you. If I ask you to come, you should come. And don't doubt my intentions either. I swear upon your son.'

With not much option left, she agreed to go with him, thinking she could show him just two or three of the eight to ten pots that were buried. She handed over the child to her neighbour Kamalavva and said, 'There is no way we can hide things, avva. Tell my husband whatever has happened. Please look after this child.'

'Show him the buried pots and come back soon. Let them be broken. What else can we do?' The old woman gave her some confidence. Rukki gave a tight hug to her child, kissed it on the chin, said, 'I will be back, very soon my child,' and got into the car.

The car began to move in the direction where the pots were buried, but all of a sudden, the car changed its course. As it was negotiating a steep road on the hillside, the car began to slow down. Rukki began to doubt his intentions. For some reason, the car came to a sudden halt. Rukki immediately jumped out and began to run. Rangaraju came out of the car and ran after her. Without knowing what to do, she ran towards the edge of the cliff. He began to drag her towards him. When both of them got to the edge, she must have decided what to do. She gathered all her strength and gave him a push. As he must have been holding her hand tightly, both of them fell into the deep gorge and lost their lives.

By the time Limbya got back home from Nagarkote, the police had released Duglibai and Damla's wife after beating them without mercy. The old woman in the neighbouring house told Limbya everything that had happened. Limbya, Dhenya, Khubya and I went looking for the car with torches in our hand. After searching everywhere, around early morning we found their dead bodies.

This news spread across the Thanda. Somalya who was already disturbed mentally was shocked by this incident. He felt sorry to know the fate of Rukki who was looked after by him as his own daughter. 'Wicked worm, wicked worm, cruel creature,' he would shout for a while and then he would murmur, 'the ten-headed demon has let loose his terror.' Anyone would be moved to sorrow looking at Duglibai weeping and beating her chest, bitterly cursing the man who was responsible for her daughter's death. As the body was consigned to flames, Limbya wept inconsolably. We had to console him as best as we could. Somalya embraced Limbya and began to weep more loudly than him. Now we had to pacify Somalya, leaving aside Limbya.

All preparation in connection with Holi was suspended while the last rites of Rukki were in progress. People who came for the last ceremony praised Rukki and this brought Limbya and Duglibai to tears. Kamlibai, the old woman next door, composed a hoonasathi – a song sung in praise of a woman who has martyred herself to save her honour – and sang it. The song narrated the love affair between Rukki and Limbya, her regrets, their marriage, her life as a devoted wife, the way she had entrusted the child to her and how she managed to take the life of the wicked man who wanted to play with her modesty. She said raping Rukki was akin to raping the forest fairy. There was not a single person who listened to this piteous narration and did not shed tears. Everyone appreciated Kamlibai's song, except Thukya, Loku's confidante, who remarked rather sarcastically, 'The brakes on Rangaraju's car must have failed and slipped while negotiating a turn, causing the car to fall into the gorge killing both of them. People are unnecessarily weaving a heroic story around this.' Nobody took his comments seriously. He was given to such sarcasm; he was one who would find stones in curd. It did not matter how they died, but the fact remains that it upset all of us very badly.

Madali, a special sweet dish, was made for the last day of the ceremony. Everyone was given a madali laddu to eat. Somalya Nayak was asked to feed the little eight-month-old child a couple of grains of madali. 'What can I say? They call me an elderly person. How am I an elderly person? A useless elder,' he said and began to laugh out loud. Some people began to say, 'Why did you ask him to speak? He is not sound in mind.' Later, Somalya became serious and said, 'Grandson, grow up to be a great person. Become a neem tree, become a tree...what else can I say? Light a green lamp, build a lake.' So saying, he fed the child a few grains of madali; the child began to laugh with its toothless mouth wide open.

On learning that Somalya had come back to the Thanda, Basappa master came to meet him. 'I have never been able to take the Thanda off my mind though a lot of water has flown under the bridge,' he said. I took him home and despite my insistence that he have lunch, he refused saying that he had already eaten in Kalluru, and that he would just have some tea. After a casual conversation, he began to remark with awe at the changes that had taken place in the Thanda in the last three or four years. 'There are good hotels near the Kalluru bus stop. I didn't find the women who used to sell chiku fruits stacked in their baskets. Several women would come to the windows of the buses and sell the fruit shouting, "Chikus! Chikus!" When I inquired I got to know that a company had been set up to make juice out of chiku and the juice was being packed in sealed bottles and exported out of the country. I believe the company is doing good business.

I also saw a few granite polishing companies scattered across the place. When I reached the Thanda I was shocked to see that the hills had disappeared along with the trees, the shrubs and the stream. No human can raise the hills! Pity, things that had existed for over a thousand years have been destroyed in a matter of three years! What do we leave behind for our future generation? I remember the days when I strolled around in the hills and forests, eating fruits and berries! Wherever I look, I find heaps of dust in place of hillocks. If I feel so bad, I can understand how hurt the feelings of Somalya would be.' The teacher went on telling me many more things. He enquired about Loku, Zimri and Rukki. When I told him about them he felt sad and troubled. I had already informed him about Somalya. 'If he recognizes one occasionally, he speaks to them. Even when he speaks, he is not coherent; you should not mind this.'

When we went to Somalya's house, he was seated on the porch, talking to himself. I told him, 'Basappa master has come to meet you.' He held the teacher's hand firmly and let it go. Then he raised his hands skyward and looked up. He did not utter a word. He just sat there silently. 'This is how he behaves,' I said. When the teacher spoke to Rupli who was lying down inside the house, coughing and wheezing, there were tears in her eyes. When he saw Zimri, he remarked, 'Zimri is no longer her former self. How thin she has become!' He had to go back the same day. I went to see him off.

'We say Somalya has lost his mental balance,' said Basappa master. 'I don't know whether we are right or wrong. How is it that man has been exploiting and devastating nature in his desire to gain wealth? How hurt he must have been to be a witness to such destruction! He must have been so pained and deeply hurt on seeing me that he could not utter a single word!' I sighed, nodding my head and mumbling my assent, and bid goodbye to Basappa master.

Two more lodges were under construction in Kalluru and people from the Thanda were going there as labourers. Zimri went there to do construction work to provide for her asthmatic mother and lame husband. Sometimes, people would ask her, 'Your brother is quite well-to-do. Where is the need for you to toil as a labourer?' She would give a crisp response, 'What he has earned is his, and what is my due is mine.' Once in a while, I would go there and help Somalya's family with some food grain. Looking at Zimri serving her, Rupli would become sad and say, 'You have not yet been freed from troubles.'

One night, her wheezing became uncontrollable. She felt like she was choking and was unable to breathe. She was suffering a lot. We gave her all the treatment that we were aware of. Somebody went and informed Loku. By the time he arrived, she had recovered so well that there were no signs of her having suffered. In spite of that he said, 'I will take you to the hospital in Nagarkote. Be ready.' She responded rather strongly, 'I don't want to go there. I don't like the treatment provided in the hospital. Let the divine wish of Mariyamma prevail.' I continued to stay put even after the rest of the people had left. Rupli looked at me and her daughter, wept bitterly and said, 'Look after him. I don't know when I will breathe my last.'

'He is a great man!' Somalya said, 'Who knows who will die first and who later! We got together after we were born here. Similarly, we will also depart from here at different times.' Though he spoke these consoling words, he was not at peace with himself.

They gathered firewood from every possible place for the Holi bonfire. They made a fifteen feet tall idol of Kamanna (Kama). By dawn, the idol would be set on fire and boys would begin to revel. Somalya didn't seem to have had a wink of sleep the previous night. Either because of the merriment and noise created by the boys outside, or because of his own internal disturbances, Somalya could not get any sleep. He was present when the idol of Kama was set on fire. All the young boys and girls gathered around the idol of Kama. When the fire was lit, the flames rose sky high and began to burn brightly. Somalya, who was standing nearby began to shout, 'Fire! Fire!' There was nothing surprising about this. Because there indeed was fire. But he continued to shout 'Fire! Fire!' even after reaching home. He removed his turban, shirt and other clothing and began to jump as if he had been set on fire.

'Everything has been burnt to ashes,' he began to say. When I went to his house, Somalya was still perturbed. 'It could be the curse of Mariyamma. Take him to the temples of Sevalal and Mariyamma,' Ruplibai requested. She continued, 'Who knows what thoughts have been eating away at him from within! When Loku was young, he was such a doted child of ours; why has he become like this! He is intelligent, he is capable, but why did he become like this! I will offer my prayers to god to give him good sense.' She shed tears. I approached Somalya who was sitting on the porch outside and said to him, 'Come let us go out for a walk.'

'I don't want to. I will stay here,' he said, rather stubbornly. I thought it was not appropriate to force him and quietly went back home.

On returning from the fields, I would freshen up, have some tea and visit Somalya. This had become a routine for me. He was seated lost in some thought on the porch. He remained silent though I went on speaking to him. A little later, he lifted his head and asked, 'When did you come?...A demon has been wreaking havoc in the Thanda. He has been spreading his tentacles in every direction. The reach of his hands is so long that they extend up to several leagues. He is not satisfied with anything. He swallows all the available stones, lakes of water, plants and trees and still looks for more. Strangely, this fellow has no head or heart, he just has a huge stomach – a large drum-like belly. Mother earth has been crying unbearably!' I didn't know why he was telling me this story! 'Yes, let us accept the fact that such a demon has entered our place; what should we do now?' I asked him. 'There is nothing we can do. Let us pray to Sevalal.' So saying, he began to clap his hands and sing.

> *The giant belches after gobbling up,*
> *Eats stone, mud and lake;*
> *Swallows even the wind that blows,*
> *Sevalal, you alone can save us.*

The sun is burning bright,
The moon is shedding blood;
Mother earth is shivering,
Sevalal, you alone can save us.

Let the race of the demons be destroyed;
Let all other forms of life survive;
Let the generations prosper;
Come Sevalal, save us.

He was engrossed in singing and clapping, praying to Sevalal. I just sat there, not knowing what to do. Later, I took advantage of the situation and suggested, 'Come, let's go to the temples of Sevalal and Mariyamma.' He abruptly got up, ready to go. We started walking towards the new temples built for Sevalal and Mariyamma next to the road leading to the hills. Trucks and tractors were passing by, honking horns and raising a lot of dust and noise. The sounds of the earlier days when one could hear Somalya's bhajan accompanied with the sound of bells and the chirping of birds in the trees had been washed away. The saffron flag atop the newly built cement temple was fluttering like the wings of a wounded pigeon. I suppressed all my feelings within myself, whatever they were, and went to offer my prayers to Sevalal. 'Sevalal, please help Somalya recover,' I prayed and entered the temple. Somalya stepped into the temple for the first time.

It had well-laid granite flooring; the doors were also covered with granite stone that was shining brightly. There were tubelights to illuminate the inside. The idol of Sevalal was made of silver. Mr Desai believed that he had prospered largely because of the blessings of these gods and hence had personally appointed a priest to both the temples.

As we were entering, Somalya saw this temple and was taken aback. 'Where is Sevalal? He is not here. This is not a temple,' he began to shout loudly. 'I don't want this, I don't want this,' he said and went out and sat down. 'Be seated here,' I said and went into the temple. When the priest asked me, 'Why is the man shouting like that?' I said, 'He is not mentally sound.' When he asked, 'Who is he?' I told him, 'He was the chief of this Thanda, and now he has become like this.'

The priest went in and recited some hymns and performed the aarathi. I joined my hands in respect and made an offering of some change that was in my pocket. The priest gave me some flowers that had been offered to the god. I packed a little of the sacred ash in a piece of paper and came out with the ash and flowers in my hand. But Somalya was not there where I had left him. I felt concerned.

Since it was getting dark, things were not clearly visible. I could make out a figure at a distance, going towards the hills. I realized it was Somalya and hurried towards him. He began to climb the hill. I shouted out in a frightened voice, 'Oh, Somalya, come back, let's go. The workers would have placed dynamites in the stones before going home in the evening. It may explode! Come down,' I continued to shout. He shouted back, 'Yes, the stones are burning...the mud is burning...the lake is burning... everything is burning fiercely...come let us put out these flames.'

Hearing my shouts, a few others had come and gathered around the place. By then, Somalya had entered the quarry. All of a sudden, there was an explosion and Somalya was thrown up, torn to pieces. All the people around came and held me back me as I tried to rush towards him. They did not let go of me till a few more dynamites had exploded and the stones had broken into small pieces. After the explosions subsided, I went to Somalya and found his head severed from his body and the torso lying in different places. Loku came and said, 'My father never recovered his senses. He brought this end upon himself. Who can help such people?' He asked his men to put the severed parts of the body together and take it to the old house. When we took the body

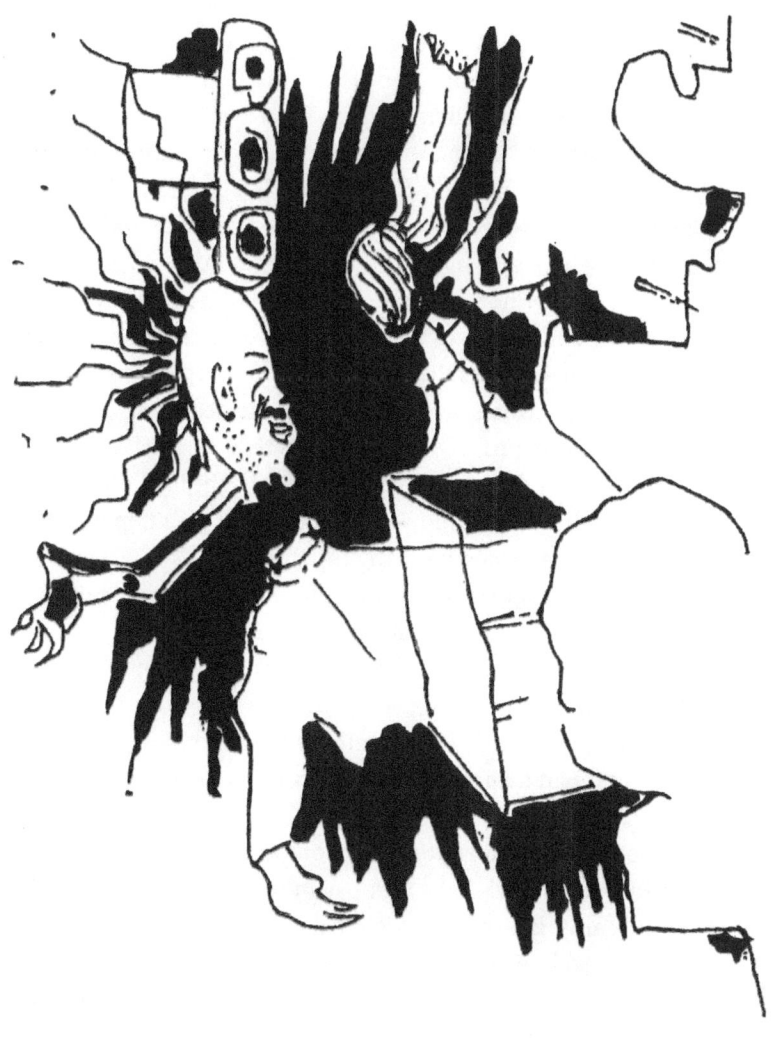

home, Rupli, Zimri, the son-in-law and the grandchild were all shocked. We once again put together the head and the body and covered it with a white sheet of cloth. Rupli wept uncontrollably, all the while singing his praises. 'I wanted to die before you. You have left me behind as your widow! I couldn't die as your wife! You would admit all your wrongs and rectify them! You were a great man! I couldn't understand you!'

Zimri touched her father's feet and cried, 'Father, do you want to leave all of us behind and go to that Sevalal! I was here because of you. I was here ready to serve you. Why did you go there, there where they had placed dynamites in the quarry?' The children, who did not understand what had happened, began to cry as their mother was crying. All the people of the Thanda gathered. Loku came and began to hurry the people along. 'Since he died of an explosion, we cannot retain the dead body for long, there will be problems. We cannot wait either for Hari or anyone else.' He ordered the bier to be prepared. Night had already set in. Besides, there was a power shutdown. Rupli's bangles, the ornaments that adorned her hair, and the arm-bands around her blouse were all stripped off her and placed on the dead body.

Since the elder son was not present, I asked Loku to come forward and carry the bier on his shoulders first. Then we started for the crematorium taking turns to carry the bier. Loku was leading the procession with an empty broken pot and another new pot that had a lamp in it. By the time we reached, firewood had been piled and kept ready. After the son lit the pyre at the head, the rest of us paid our respects one after the other. The pyre began to burn fiercely. My legs began to shiver. I wished he'd come back alive rising from this fire and the ashes.

We got back, washed ourselves and went back to Nayak's house. I just sat quietly not knowing what to say. A small lamp had been lit in the house. The flame began to flicker. Dim light lit the faces of his grandchildren.

Author's Note

I have been attracted to the Lambada tribe right from my childhood. Being curious about these neglected people, it has become a habit with me to wander around their settlements and mix with them. Through these wanderings I have been accompanied and assisted by Chennappa Katti, Padashetty, S.K. Konesagar, S.M. Kambalimath, Chowkimath, Nagaraj Nadagowda, brothers Mrityunjaya, Lingaiah, Annadaani and Gaveesh.

When I was contemplating writing the novel in Kannada, I met Mr T.S. Ranga the famous film director in a conference. He mentioned the topic of grazing grounds and encouraged me by corresponding with me regularly. I have benefitted from the writings of Dr P.K. Khandoba, Dr D.B. Nayak and Dr Harilal Pawar before beginning to write this novel.

After writing a couple of chapters, when I gave up writing due to certain inconveniences, Raghavendra Patil known for his creative writing read the manuscript. He not only expressed his wish to publish the book from his publishing house, but also persuaded me to continue writing. He also brought pressure on me from Lalitha my life partner. It is because of their love and persuasion that this novel saw the light of the day.

Dr H.S. Raghavendra Rao, Bidarhalli, Narasimha Murthy, Anand Zunzarwada, Mahesh Thippashetti have gone through the manuscript in Kannada and offered their useful comments. S. Diwakar, a well-known short story writer and one who has made world famous stories available to readers in Kannada, has often lent me books and encouraged me to write.

Caught in the administrative chores of the college, when I was hard pressed for time, my student Sangu Math offered to be my scribe. S.B. Doddamani has been of great help in proofreading the manuscript. My student Basavaraj Gavimath has sketched beautiful illustrations.My uncle Dr Panchakshari Hiremath has been a guiding force in my life and writings.

My daughter Geetha (Nirupa), son-in-law Rajesh, Usha, Paapu, Vijayashri and children have anxiously awaited the publication of the novel in Kannada. Sumeet, my grandson has captivated me with his little pranks.

I owe my gratitude to all these people and the large family of my readers.

MALLIKARJUN HIREMATH

28, Chiatanya, 1st Main
C B Nagar, Dharwad 580007
M: 9945607144
mallikarjunhiremath12@gmail.com

Translator's Note

A couple of years after Havan was published in Kannada, Hyderabad Book Trust (HBT) wanted to have the book translated into Telugu. Ms Gita Ramaswamy of HBT approached Professor Jayashree Mohanraj, who is on the panel of translators for the Sahitya Akademi. Since my familiarity with Kannada is reasonably good, Jayashree (my wife) accepted the assignment with a tacit understanding that the project would be a collaborative one. Because of the close affinity between the two languages in terms of their idiom, culture and ethos the translation did not prove to be a very difficult task.

The translation from Kannada to Telugu had us read the novel in original a few times to make ourselves familiar with the plot, narration and other details involved in writing. It was this familiarity that made me bold enough to accept the task of translating the same novel into English when I was approached by Mr Sridhar Balan of Ratna Books. Having accepted the task, I found the work to be more challenging, for English lacked some of the exact equivalents for idiomatic expressions used in Kannada and in particular terms associated with local tribes. The grammatical structures in Kannada are very different from that of English. It is possible to have a sentence in Kannada without the use of a verb. An adjective and a noun can have the full purport of a sentence. While translating such sentences, and also some of the longer constructions, attempt was made to translate the sentences without altering their structure. This either made the sentences appear quaint or un-English. In this process of translation, the author, Sri Mallikarjun Hiremath and Jayashree helped me to a great extent in refining my draft and rendering it in the present form. I owe my gratitude to both of them.

Excerpts from two seminal write-ups about this novel in Kannada by Dr C.N. Ramachandran and Dr T.P. Ashok appear on the jacket of the book. My sincere thanks to both of them.

Despite all the help I have received, the book may still have a few unacceptable sentences and inappropriate translations. I take responsibility for all these and welcome any suggestions and comments from the readers.

S. MOHANRAJ

SM 50, Saket Mithila, Saket
Kapra, Hyderabad 500062
M: 9849993439
mohanrajsathuvalli@gmail.com